T0347600

SCENES OF
LONDON LIFE

Complete & Unabridged

George Cruikshank

LONDON RECREATIONS

CHARLES DICKENS

SCENES OF
LONDON LIFE

FROM *Sketches by Boz*

Selected and introduced by
J. B. PRIESTLEY

With illustrations by
GEORGE CRUIKSHANK

MACMILLAN COLLECTOR'S LIBRARY

Sketches by Boz first published 1839

This selection first published 1947 by Pan Books

This edition published by Macmillan Collector's Library 2018
an imprint of Pan Macmillan
The Smithson, 6 Briset Street, London EC1M 5NR
EU representative: Macmillan Publishers Ireland Ltd,
1st Floor, The Liffey Trust Centre, 117–126 Sheriff Street Upper,
Dublin 1, DO1 YC43
Associated companies throughout the world
www.panmacmillan.com

ISBN 978-1-5098-5428-8

Introduction © J. B. Priestley 1947

5 7 9 8 6 4

A CIP catalogue record for this book is available from the British Library.

Casing design and endpaper pattern by Andrew Davidson
Typeset by Ellipsis, Glasgow
Printed and bound in China by Imago

Visit www.panmacmillan.com to read more about all our books
and to buy them. You will also find features, author interviews and
news of any author events, and you can sign up for e-newsletters
so that you're always first to hear about our new releases.

Contents

Illustrations

Introduction

J. B. PRIESTLEY

One afternoon, towards the end of the year 1833, a
shabby young reporter, on his way to the House of
Commons, stopped at 186 Strand, the shop of Messrs.
Chapman and Hall, and paid a precious half-crown for
the current issue of the *Monthly Magazine*. There was
nothing sensational about this periodical, which had
recently been acquired, for £300, by a certain Captain
Holland, newly arrived from South America. Yet the
young reporter might have been seen holding his copy
of the *Monthly Magazine* with a shaking hand, and
staring at its pages with eyes blazing with excitement
and afterwards filling with tears. There, secure and
glorious for ever in print, was one of his Sketches—"A
Dinner in Poplar Walk." Charles Dickens had begun his
literary career.

There was only one thing wrong with this *Monthly
Magazine*. It was pleased to accept this unknown reporter as a frequent contributor of Sketches of London
life. But it could not pay for them. The gallant Captain
Holland, who had fought with Bolivar, could offer print
and glory but no money. (Eighteen months afterwards
he sold the magazine at a profit.) And young Dickens
needed money. He had as yet no wife and family to
keep, but he had a father who was definitely a financial
liability and not an asset.

His prospects, however, soon brightened. In 1835,
as "the fastest and most accurate man in the (Press)
Gallery," he was engaged by the *Morning Chronicle* at

five guineas a week, which, when we remember what money could buy in those days, we must consider a surprisingly handsome salary. But then Dickens, though only twenty-three, was no ordinary reporter. There seems no reason to doubt his own claim, often made afterwards, that he was the best reporter in the country. When the House was sitting, he reported it regularly; but he was also sent up and down the country as what we should call now a Special Correspondent, to report by-elections, special meetings, and various events of national importance. He showed great ingenuity in devising ways of delivering his "copy" at full speed, and enjoyed himself immensely tearing round the country. And before we see him established as an author, we ought to consider him a little longer in his capacity as a star reporter, if only because this young man helps us to understand the great novelist he soon became.

To be a successful fast stenographer, as young Dickens was, a man has to turn himself into a machine. This requires a considerable effort of will on anybody's part, but the effort of will demanded from Dickens, with his particular temperament, must have been appalling. But this high-spirited imaginative lad who applied himself to shorthand was determined never to sink again to the blacking-factory level. He was compact of energy, determination, will.

There was no stopping him. He would be the best reporter in England, and within a few years, while still hardly more than a mere boy, he *was* the best reporter in England. The point is important. We are so used to thinking of Dickens as a mercurial creature who over-indulged his temperament, moods and whims, as a restless and dissatisfied man, alternating between sudden melancholy and uproarious high spirits, that we are apt to overlook the significant fact that from the first, when he applied himself so grimly to short-hand, to the last, when he struggled on to his reading platforms against all his doctors' orders, he was a man of powerful will, capable of the most ferocious self-discipline. The amount of work he did, including the amazing number of long letters he wrote, proves this. And the temperamental moody Dickens, who was really making holiday, should be seen against this lifelong story of unrelaxed effort.

Again, it has been a familiar criticism of Dickens as a novelist that he really did not know enough, that his experience and observation of life were very limited. But to make this criticism is to overlook his brief but very successful career as a reporter. Here is a man who began his literary life by haunting the Houses of Parliament and the Law Courts and making profes-sional journeys to innumerable provincial places. And if, for example, he was for ever afterwards either wildly or grimly satirical in his handling of politicians and lawyers, it simply will not do to defend them and attack him by declaring that he wrote out of sheer ignorance.

It is true that he did not know or care enough about Politics and the Law in their majestic but abstract forms, and from this point of view he can be sharply criticised. But what he did know, from actual experi-ence, was how politicians and lawyers really behaved, and he refused to be humbugged by the solemn trappings of the scene. (As nearly everybody else is, by the way.) Thus, there is much in Parliament that Dickens missed, but it is equally true to say that there is a pompous silliness about much of our Parliamentary proceedings that Dickens saw at once and afterwards hit off to perfection. The same may be said of the Law Courts. His satire, deliberately wild and grotesque as it often is, probably comes far nearer to the truth than anything we can find in the portentous memoirs of politicians and judges. What he saw, he saw with a fresh, keen, young eye, unglazed by habit and custom. And he saw a great deal. He was not a star reporter for nothing.

The type of Sketches he had been contributing gratis to the *Monthly Magazine* were suitable for newspapers too, and when the *Evening Chronicle* came into existence, under the same management as the morning paper that employed him, he became one of its contributors and had his salary raised to seven guineas a week. Young Dickens could now sport a new hat and a fine blue cloak with black velvet facings. He was now a real author, and contributed "Scenes and Characters"—twelve of them under the very Dickensian name of "Tibbs"—to *Bell's Life in London*. But for most of his Sketches he had borrowed the family nursery name of a brother—"Boz." And now "Boz" began to be talked about. Harrison Ainsworth, a dashing young man who had already made a hit with his *Rookwood*, invited young Dickens to his Sunday afternoon parties at Kensal Lodge, Willesden, then a village outside London. It was there that Dickens met the publisher Macrone, and it was Macrone who suggested that Dickens should assemble his Sketches for publication as a book, to be illustrated by Cruikshank.

There was some delay in bringing out the book, chiefly because Cruikshank was behind time with his illustrations. Finally it appeared, on the author's twenty-fourth birthday, as *Sketches by Boz: Illustrative of Every Day Life and Every Day People*. Macrone paid a hundred and fifty pounds for the book, a sum that would probably be worth more than six hundred pounds now. We are apt to imagine that young authors are much better off in these days than they were a hundred years ago, but all the hard facts are against such an assumption. Dickens could afford to marry and set up a tiny establishment on what he received for his first book, a work of non-fiction by an almost unknown author. It is not likely that any similar young writer could do that to-day. Our progress in this field is very doubtful.

Sketches by Boz was warmly received, as well it might be, although its modest success was soon forgotten when *Pickwick* burst upon the world. It is unmistakably a young man's work. There is in it both the heavy solemnity and the rather shrill satire of youth. The descriptive sketches, as distinct from the tales, represent Dickens the reporter and not Dickens the novelist, the Dickens whose towns and streets and taverns and houses have an extra and fantastic dimension, because they are seen with the light of the unconscious as well as that of the writer's conscious mind. But here in these sketches it is sheer observation and not creative fantasy that is doing the work. This is the London of William IV. It is doubtful if we can get closer to that London than we can in these pages. Although these pieces are of special interest just because they are the earliest work of a man of genius, the reader might be well advised to try reading them without reference to what is Dickensian in them, as if they were by some unknown social commentator, or were so many peepholes through which we can obtain a glimpse of the London of the early Eighteen-Thirties.

The Sketches here have been selected to represent both Dickens, and Cruikshank, and as far as was possible to divide the honours between them. They have also been chosen to show us the London of their day, and, within the limits of so small a selection, to offer us as much variety as could be found within such limits. This little book does not pretend to be a substitute for the full fat *Sketches by Boz*. It is a Christmas appetiser and reminder: a sherry and a sardine before the great Dickensian feast.

Public Dinners

All public dinners in London, from the Lord Mayor's annual banquet at Guildhall, to the Chimney-sweepers' anniversary at White Conduit House; from the Goldsmiths' to the Butchers', from the Sheriffs' to the Licensed Victuallers'; are amusing scenes. Of all entertainments of this description, however, we think the annual dinner of some public charity is the most amusing. At a Company's dinner, the people are nearly all alike—regular old stagers, who make it a matter of business, and a thing not to be laughed at. At a political dinner, everybody is disagreeable, and inclined to speechify—much the same thing, by the bye; but at a charity dinner you see people of all sorts, kinds, and descriptions. The wine may not be remarkably special, to be sure, and we have heard some hard-hearted monsters grumble at the collection; but we really think the amusement to be derived from the occasion sufficient to counterbalance even these disadvantages.

Let us suppose you are induced to attend a dinner of this description—"Indigent Orphans' Friends' Benevolent Institution," we think it is. The name of the charity is a line or two longer, but never mind the rest. You have a distinct recollection, however, that you purchased a ticket at the solicitation of some charitable friend: and you deposit yourself in a hackney-coach, the driver of which—no doubt that you may do the thing in style—turns a deaf ear to your earnest entreaties to be set down at the corner of Great Queen Street, and persists in carrying you to the very door of the Freemasons', round which a crowd of people are assembled to witness the entrance of the indigent orphans' friends. You hear great speculations as you pay the fare, on the possibility of your being the noble Lord who is announced to fill the chair on the occasion, and are highly gratified to hear it eventually decided that you are only a "wocalist."

The first thing that strikes you, on your entrance, is the astonishing importance of the committee. You observe a door on the first landing, carefully guarded by two waiters, in and out of which stout gentlemen with very red faces keep running, with a degree of speed highly unbecoming the gravity of persons of their years and corpulency. You pause, quite alarmed at the bustle, and thinking, in your innocence, that two or three people must have been carried out of the dining-room in fits, at least. You are immediately undeceived by the waiter—"Upstairs, if you please, sir; this is the committee-room." Upstairs you go, accordingly; wondering, as you mount, what the duties of the committee can be, and whether they ever do anything beyond confusing each other, and running over the waiters.

Having deposited your hat and cloak, and received a remarkably small scrap of pasteboard in exchange (which, as a matter of course, you lose before you require it again), you enter the hall, down which there are three long tables for the less distinguished guests, with a cross-table on a raised platform at the upper end for the reception of the very particular friends of the indigent orphans. Being fortunate enough to find a plate without anybody's card in it, you wisely seat yourself at once, and have a little leisure to look about you. Waiters, with wine-baskets in their hands, are placing decanters of sherry down the tables, at very respectable distances; melancholy-looking salt-cellars, and decayed vinegar-cruets, which might have belonged to the parents of the indigent orphans in their time, are scattered at distant intervals on the cloth; and the knives and forks look as if they had done duty at every public dinner in London since the accession of George the First. The musicians are scraping and grating and screwing tremendously—playing no notes but notes of preparation; and several gentlemen are gliding along the sides of the tables, looking into plate after plate with frantic eagerness, the expression of their countenances growing more and more dismal as they meet with everybody's card but their own.

You turn round to take a look at the table behind you, and—not being in the habit of attending public dinners—are somewhat struck by the appearance of the party on which your eyes rest. One of its principal members appears to be a little man, with a long and rather inflamed face, and grey hair brushed bolt upright in front; he wears a wisp of black silk round his neck, without any stiffener, as an apology for a neckerchief, and is addressed by his companions by the familiar appellation of "Fitz," or some much monosyllable. Near him is a stout man in a white neckerchief and buff waistcoat, with shining dark hair, cut very short in front, and a great round healthy-looking face, on which he studiously preserves a half-sentimental simper. Next him, again, is a large-headed man, with black hair and bushy whiskers; and opposite them are two or three others, one of whom is a little round-faced person, in a dress-stock and blue under-waistcoat. There is something peculiar in their air and manner, though you could hardly describe what it is; you cannot divest yourself of the idea that they have come for some other purpose than mere eating and drinking. You have no time to debate the matter, however, for the waiters (who have been arranged in lines down the room, placing the dishes on table) retire to the lower end; the dark man in the blue coat and bright buttons, who has the direction of the music, looks up to the gallery, and calls out "band" in a very loud voice; out burst the orchestra, up rise the visitors, in march fourteen stewards, each with a long wand, in his hand, like the evil genius in a pantomime; then the chairman, then the titled visitors; they all make their way up the room, as fast as they can, bowing, and smiling, and smirking, and looking remarkably amiable. The applause ceases, grace is said, the clatter of plates and dishes begins; and every one appears highly gratified, either with the presence of the distinguished visitors, or the commencement of the anxiously-expected dinner.

As to the dinner itself—the mere dinner—it goes off much the same everywhere. Tureens of soup are emptied with awful rapidity—waiters take plates of turbot away, to get lobster-sauce, and bring back plates of lobster-sauce without turbot; people who can carve poultry are great fools if they own it, and people who can't have no wish to learn. The knives and forks form a pleasing accompaniment to Auber's music, and Auber's music would form a pleasing accompaniment to the dinner, if you could hear anything besides the cymbals. The substantials disappear—moulds of jelly vanish like lightning—hearty eaters wipe their foreheads, and appear rather overcome by their recent exertions—people who have looked very cross hitherto, become remarkably bland, and ask you to take wine in the most friendly manner possible—old gentlemen direct your attention to the ladies' gallery, and take great pains to impress you with the fact that the charity is always peculiarly favoured in this respect—everyone appears disposed to become talkative—and the hum of conversation is loud and general.

"Pray, silence, gentlemen, if you please, for *Non nobis!*" shouts the toastmaster with stentorian lungs—a toastmaster's shirt-front, waistcoat, and neckerchief, by the by, always exhibit three distinct shades of cloudy-white—"Pray, silence, gentlemen, for *Non nobis!*" The singers, whom you discover to be no other than the very party that excited your curiosity at first, after "pitching" their voices immediately begin *too-too*ing most dismally, on which the regular old stagers burst into occasional cries of—"Sh—Sh—waiters!—Silence, waiters—stand still, waiters—keep back, waiters," and other exorcisms, delivered in a tone of indignant remonstrance. The grace is soon concluded, and the company resume their seats. The uninitiated portion of the guests applaud *Non nobis* as vehemently as if it were a capital comic song, greatly to the scandal and indignation of the regular diners, who immediately attempt to quell this sacrilegious approbation, by cries of "Hush, hush!" whereupon the others, mistaking these sounds for hisses, applaud more tumultuously, than before, and, by way of placing their approval beyond the possibility of doubt, shout *"Encore!"* most vociferously.

The moment the noise ceases, up starts the toastmaster:—"Gentlemen, charge your glasses, if you please!" Decanters having been handed about, and glasses filled, the toastmaster proceeds, in a regular ascending scale:—"Gentlemen—*air*—you—all charged? Pray—silence—gentlemen—for—the cha—i—r!" The

George Cruikshank

PUBLIC DINNERS

chairman rises, and, after stating that he feels it quite unnecessary to preface the toast he is about to propose, with any observations whatever, wanders into, a maze of sentences, and flounders about in the most extraordinary manner, presenting a lamentable spectacle of mystified humanity, until he arrives at the words, "constitutional sovereign of these realms," at which elderly gentlemen exclaim "Bravo!" and hammer the table tremendously with their knife-handles. "Under any circumstances, it would give him the greatest pride, it would give him the greatest pleasure—he might almost say, it would afford him satisfaction [cheers] to propose that toast. What must be his feelings, then, when he has the gratification of announcing, that he has received her Majesty's commands to apply to the Treasurer of her Majesty's Household, for her Majesty's annual donation of 25*l*, in aid of the funds of this charity!" This announcement (which has been regularly made by every chairman, since the first foundation of the charity, forty-two years ago) calls forth the most vociferous applause; the toast is drunk with a great deal of cheering and knocking; and "God save the Queen" is sung by the "professional gentlemen"; the unprofessional gentlemen joining in the chorus, and giving the national anthem an effect which the newspapers, with great justice, describe as "perfectly electrical."

The other "loyal and patriotic" toasts having been drunk with all due enthusiasm, a comic song having been well sung by the gentleman with the small neckerchief, and a sentimental one by the second of the party, we come to the most important toast of the evening—"Prosperity to the charity." Here again we are compelled to adopt newspaper phraseology, and to express our regret at being "precluded from giving even the substance of the noble lord's observations." Suffice it to say, that the speech, which is somewhat of the longest, is rapturously received; and the toast having been drunk, the stewards (looking more important than ever) leave the room, and presently return, heading a procession of indigent orphans, boys and girls, who walk round the room, curtseying, and bowing, and treading on each other's heels, and looking very much as if they would like a glass of wine a-piece, to the high gratification of the company generally, and especially of the lady patronesses in the gallery. *Exeunt* children, and re-enter stewards, each with a blue plate in his hand. The band plays a lively air; the majority of the company put their hands in their pockets and look rather serious; and the noise of sovereigns, rattling on crockery, is heard from all parts of the room.

After a short interval, occupied in singing and toasting, the secretary puts on his spectacles, and proceeds to read the report and list of subscriptions, the latter being listened to with great attention. "Mr. Smith, one guinea—Mr. Tompkins, one guinea—Mr. Wilson, one guinea—Mr. Hickson, one guinea—Mr. Nixon, one guinea—Mr. Charles Nixon, one guinea—[hear, hear!]—Mr. James Nixon, one guinea—Mr. Thomas Nixon, one pound one [tremendous applause]. Lord Fitz Binkle, the chairman of the day, in addition to an annual donation of fifteen pounds—thirty guineas [prolonged knocking: several gentlemen knock the stems off their wine-glasses, in the vehemence of their approbation], Lady Fitz Binkle, in addition to an annual donation of ten pound—twenty pound" [protracted knocking and shouts of "Bravo!"]. The list being at length concluded, the chairman rises, and proposes the health of the secretary, than whom he knows no more zealous or estimable individual. The secretary, in returning thanks, observes that *he* knows no more excellent individual than the chairman—except the senior officer of the charity, whose health *he* begs to propose. The senior officer, in returning thanks, observes that *he* knows no more worthy man than the secretary—except Mr. Walker, the auditor, whose health *he* begs to propose. Mr. Walker, in returning thanks, discovers some other estimable individual, to whom alone the senior officer is inferior—and so they go on toasting and lauding and thanking: the only other toast of importance being "The Lady Patronesses now present!" on which all the gentlemen turn their faces towards the ladies' gallery, shouting tremendously; and little priggish men, who have imbibed more wine than usual, kiss their hands and exhibit distressing contortions of visage.

We have protracted our dinner to so great a length, that we have hardly time to add one word by way of grace. We can only entreat our readers not to imagine, because we have attempted to extract some amusement from a charity dinner, that we are at all disposed to under-rate, either the excellence of the benevolent institutions with which London abounds, or the estimable motives of those who support them.

Shops and Their Tenants

What inexhaustible food for speculation, do the streets
of London afford! We never were able to agree with
Sterne in pitying the man who could travel from Dan
to Beersheba, and say that all was barren; we have not
the slightest commiseration for the man who can take
up his hat and stick, and walk from Covent Garden to
St. Paul's Churchyard, and back into the bargain,
without deriving some amusement—we had almost
said instruction—from his perambulation. And yet
there are such beings: we meet them every day. Large
black stocks and light waistcoats, jet canes and dis-
contented countenances, are the characteristics of the
race; other people brush quickly by you, steadily
plodding on to business, or cheerfully running after
pleasure. These men linger listlessly past, looking as
happy and animated as a policeman on duty. Nothing
seems to make an impression on their minds: nothing
short of being knocked down by a porter, or run over
by a cab, will disturb their equanimity. You will meet
them on a fine day in any of the leading thoroughfares
peep through the window of a west-end cigar shop in
the evening, if you can manage to get a glimpse
between the blue curtains which intercept the vulgar
gaze, and you see them in their only enjoyment of
existence. There they are lounging about, on round
tubs and pipe boxes, in all the dignity of whiskers, and
gilt watch-guards; whispering soft nothings to the
young lady in amber, with the large earrings, who, as

she sits behind the counter in a blaze of adoration and gas-light, is the admiration of all the female servants in the neighbourhood, and the envy of every milliner's apprentice within two miles round.

One of our principal amusements is to watch the gradual progress—the rise or fall—of particular shops. We have formed an intimate acquaintance with several, in different parts of town, and are perfectly acquainted with their whole history. We could name off-hand twenty at least, which we are quite sure have paid no taxes for the last six years. They are never inhabited for more than two months consecutively, and, we verily believe, have witnessed every retail trade in the Directory.

There is one, whose history is a sample of the rest, in whose fate we have taken especial interest, having had the pleasure of knowing it ever since it has been a shop. It is on the Surrey side of the water—a little distance beyond the Marsh Gate. It was originally a substantial, good-looking private house enough; the landlord got into difficulties, the house got into Chancery, the tenant went away, and the house went to ruin. At this period our acquaintance with it commenced; the paint was all worn off; the windows were broken, the area was green with neglect and the overflowings of the water-butt; the butt itself was without a lid, and the street-door was the very picture of misery. The chief pastime of the children in the vicinity had been to assemble in a body on the steps, and to take it in turn to knock loud double-knocks at the door, to the great satisfaction of the neighbours generally, and especially of the nervous old lady next door but one. Numerous complaints were made, and several small basins of water discharged over the offenders, but without effect. In this state of things, the marine-store dealer at the corner of the street, in the most obliging manner took the knocker off, and sold it: and the unfortunate house looked more wretched than ever.

We deserted our friend for a few weeks. What was our surprise, on our return, to find no trace of its existence! In its place was a handsome shop, fast approaching to a state of completion, and on the shutters were large bills, informing the public that it would shortly be opened with "an extensive stock of linendrapery and haberdashery." It opened in due course; there was the name of the proprietor "and Co." in gilt letters, almost too dazzling to look at. Such ribbons and shawls! and two such elegant young men behind the counter, each in a clean collar and white neckcloth, like the lover in a farce. As to the proprietor, he did nothing but walk up and down the shop, and hand seats to the ladies, and hold important conversations with the handsomest of the young men, who was shrewdly suspected by the neighbours to be the "Co." We saw all this with sorrow; we felt a fatal presentiment that the shop was doomed—and so it was. Its decay was slow, but sure. Tickets gradually appeared in the windows; then rolls of flannel, with labels on them, were stuck outside the door; then a bill was pasted on the street-door, intimating that the first-floor was to let *un*furnished; then one of the young men disappeared altogether, and the other took to a black neckerchief, and the proprietor took to drinking. The shop became dirty, broken panes of glass remained unmended, and the stock disappeared piece-meal. At last the company's man came to cut off the water, and then the linendraper cut off himself, leaving the landlord his compliments and the key.

The next occupant was a fancy stationer. The shop

was more modestly painted than before, still it was neat; but somehow we always thought, as we passed, that it looked like a poor and struggling concern. We wished the man well, but we trembled for his success. He was a widower evidently, and had employment elsewhere, for he passed us every morning on his road to the City. The business was carried on by his eldest daughter. Poor girl! she needed no assistance. We occasionally caught a glimpse of two or three children, in mourning like herself, as they sat in the little parlour behind the shop; and we never passed at night without seeing the eldest girl at work, either for them, or in making some elegant little trifle for sale. We often thought, as her pale face looked more sad and pensive in the dim candle-light, that if those thoughtless females who interfere with, the miserable market of poor creatures such as these, knew but one-half of the misery they suffer, and the bitter privations they endure, in their honourable attempts to earn a scanty subsistence, they would, perhaps, resign even opportunities for the gratification of vanity, and an immodest love of self-display, rather than drive them to a last dreadful resource, which it would shock the delicate feelings of these *charitable* ladies to hear named.

But we are forgetting the shop. Well, we continued to watch it, and every day showed too clearly the increasing poverty of its inmates. The children were clean, it is true, but their clothes were threadbare and shabby; no tenant had been procured for the upper part of the house, from the letting of which a portion of the means of paying the rent was to have been derived, and a slow, wasting consumption prevented the eldest girl from continuing her exertions. Quarter-day arrived. The landlord had suffered from the extravagance of his

THE DRAPERY SHOP

ast tenant, and he had no compassion for the struggles of his successor; he put in an execution. As we passed one morning, the broker's men were removing the little furniture there was in the house, and a newly-posted bill informed us it was again "To Let." What became of the last tenant we never could learn; we believe the girl is past all suffering, and beyond all sorrow. God help her! We hope she is.

We were somewhat curious to ascertain what would be the next stage—for that the place had no chance of succeeding now, was perfectly clear. The bill was soon taken down, and some alterations were being made in the interior of the shop. We were in a fever of expectation; we exhausted conjecture—we imagined all possible trades, none of which were perfectly reconcilable with our idea of the gradual decay of the tenement. It opened, and we wondered why we had not guessed at the real state of the case before. The shop —not a large one at the best of times—had been converted into two: one was a bonnet-shape maker's, the other was opened by a tobacconist, who also dealt in walking-sticks and Sunday newspapers; the two were separated by a thin partition, covered with tawdry striped paper.

The tobacconist remained in possession longer than any tenant within our recollection. He was a red-faced, impudent, good-for-nothing dog, evidently accustomed to take things as they came, and to make the best of a bad job. He sold as many cigars as he could, and smoked the rest. He occupied the shop as long as he could make peace with the landlord, and when he could no longer live in quiet, he very coolly locked the door, and bolted himself. From this period, the two little dens have undergone innumerable changes. The tobacconist was succeeded by a theatrical hairdresser, who ornamented the window with a great variety of "characters," and terrific combats. The bonnet-shape maker gave place to a greengrocer, and the histrionic barber was succeeded, in his turn, by a tailor. So numerous have been the, changes, that we have of late done little, more than mark the peculiar but certain indications of a house being poorly inhabited. It has been progressing by almost imperceptible degrees. The occupiers of the shops have gradually given up room after room, until they have only reserved the little parlour for themselves. First there appeared a brass plate on the private door, with "Ladies' School" legibly engraved thereon; shortly afterwards we observed a second brass plate, then a bell, and then another bell.

When we paused in front of our old friend, and observed these signs of poverty, which are not to be mistaken, we thought as we turned away that the house had attained its lowest pitch of degradation. We were wrong. When we last passed it, a "dairy" was established in the area, and a party of melancholy-looking fowls were amusing themselves by running in at the front floor, and out at the back one.

LONDON RECREATIONS

The wish of persons in the humbler classes of life, to ape the manners and customs of those whom fortune has placed above them, is often the subject of remark, and not unfrequently of complaint. The inclination may, and no doubt does, exist to a great extent, among the small gentility—the would-be aristocrats—of the middle classes. Tradesmen and clerks, with fashionable novel-reading families, and circulating-library-subscribing daughters, get up small assemblies in humble imitation of Almack's, and promenade the dingy "large room" of some second-rate hotel with as much complacency as the enviable few who are privileged to exhibit their magnificence in that exclusive haunt of fashion and—foolery. Aspiring young ladies, who read flaming accounts of some "fancy fair in high life," suddenly grow desperately charitable; visions of admiration and matrimony float before their eyes; some wonderfully meritorious institution, which, by the strangest accident in the world, has never been heard of before, is discovered to be in a languishing condition: Thomson's great room, or Johnson's nursery-ground, is forthwith engaged, and the aforesaid young ladies, from mere charity, exhibit themselves for three days, from twelve to four, for the small charge of one shilling per head! With the exception of these classes of society, however, and a few weak and insignificant persons, we do not think the attempt at imitation to which we have alluded, prevails in any great degree. The different

character of the recreations of different classes ha
often afforded us amusement; and we have chosen it fo
the subject of our present sketch, in the hope that i
may possess some amusement for our readers.

If the regular City man, who leaves Lloyd's at fiv
o'clock, and drives home to Hackney, Clapton, Stam
ford Hill, or elsewhere, can be said to have any dail
recreation beyond his dinner, it is his garden. He neve
does anything to it with his own hands; but he take
great pride in it notwithstanding; and if you ar
desirous of paying your addresses to the younges
daughter, be sure to be in raptures with every flowe
and shrub it contains. If your poverty of expressio
compel you to make any distinction between the two
we would certainly recommend your bestowing mor
admiration on his garden than his wine. He alway
takes a walk round it, before he starts for town in th
morning, and is particularly anxious that the fish-pon
should be kept specially neat. If you call on him o
Sunday in summer-time, about an hour before dinner
you will find him sitting in an arm-chair, on the law
behind the house, with a straw hat on, reading
Sunday paper. A short distance from him you will mos
likely observe a handsome paroquet in a large brass
wire cage; ten to one but the two eldest girls ar
loitering in one of the side-walks accompanied by
couple of young gentlemen, who are holding parasol
over them—of course only to keep the sun off—whil
the younger children, with the under nursery-maid
are strolling listlessly about, in the shade. Beyond thes
occasions, his delight in his garden appears to aris
more from the consciousness of possession than actua
enjoyment of it. When he drives you down to dinner o
a week-day, he is rather fatigued with the occupation

of the morning, and tolerably cross into the bargain; but when the cloth is removed, and he has drank three or four glasses of his favourite port, he orders the French windows of his dining-room (which of course look into the garden) to be opened, and throwing a silk handkerchief over his head, and leaning back in his arm-chair, descants at considerable length upon its beauty, and the cost of maintaining it. This is to impress you—who are a young friend of the family—with a due sense of the excellence of the garden, and the wealth of its owner; and when he has exhausted the subject, he goes to sleep.

There is another and a very different class of men, whose recreation is their garden. An individual of this class resides some short distance from town—say in the Hampstead Road, or the Kilburn Road, or any other road where the houses are small and neat, and have little slips of back-garden. He and his wife—who is as clean and compact a little body as himself—have occupied the same house ever since he retired from business twenty years ago. They have no family. They once had a son, who died at about five years old. The child's portrait hangs over the mantelpiece in the best sitting-room, and a little cart he used to draw about is carefully preserved as a relic.

In fine weather the old gentleman is almost constantly in the garden; and when it is too wet to go into it, he will look out of the window at it, by the hour together. He has always something to do there, and you will see him digging, and sweeping, and cutting, and planting, with manifest delight. In spring time, there is no end to the sowing of seeds, and sticking little bits of wood over them, with labels, which look like epitaphs to their memory; and in the evening, when the sun has gone down, the perseverance with which he lugs a great watering-pot about is perfectly astonishing. The only other recreation he has is the newspaper, which he peruses every day, from beginning to end, generally reading the most interesting pieces of intelligence to his wife, during breakfast. The old lady is very fond of flowers, as the hyacinth-glasses in the parlour-window, and geranium-pots in the little front court, testify. She takes great pride in the garden too: and when one of the four fruit-trees produces rather a larger gooseberry than usual, it is carefully preserved under a wine-glass on the sideboard, for the edification of visitors, who are duly informed that Mr. So-and-so planted the tree which produced it, with his own hands. On a summer's evening, when the large watering-pot has been filled and emptied some fourteen times, and the old couple have quite exhausted themselves by trotting about, you will see them sitting happily together in the little summer-house, enjoying the calm and peace of the twilight, and watching the shadows as they fall upon the garden, and gradually growing thicker and more sombre, obscure the tints of their gayest flowers—no bad emblem of the years that have silently rolled over their heads, deadening in their course the brightest hues of early hopes and feelings which have long since faded away. These are their only recreations, and they require no more. They have within themselves the materials of comfort and content; and the only anxiety of each is to die before the other.

This is no ideal sketch. There *used* to be many old people of this description; their numbers may have diminished, and may decrease still more. Whether the course female education has taken of late days—

VAUXHALL GARDENS BY DAY

whether the pursuit of giddy frivolities, and empty nothings, has tended to unfit women for that quiet domestic life, in which they show far more beautifully than in the most crowded assembly, is a question we should feel little gratification in discussing: we hope not.

Let us turn now to another portion of the London population, whose recreations present about as strong a contrast as can well be conceived—we mean the Sunday pleasurers; and let us beg our readers to imagine themselves stationed by our side in some well-known rural "Tea-gardens."

The heat is intense this afternoon, and the people, of whom there are additional parties arriving every moment, look as warm as the tables which have been recently painted, and have the appearance of being red-hot. What a dust and noise! Men and women—boys and girls—sweethearts and married people—babies in arms, and children in chaises—pipes and shrimps—cigars and periwinkles—tea and tobacco. Gentlemen, in alarming waistcoats, and steel watch-guards, prom-enading about, three abreast, with surprising dignity (or as the gentleman in the next box facetiously observes, "cutting it uncommon fat!")—ladies, with great, long, white pocket-handkerchiefs like small table-cloths in their hands, chasing one another on the grass in the most playful and interesting manner, with the view of attracting the attention of the aforesaid gentlemen—husbands in perspective ordering bottles of ginger-beer for the objects of their affections, with a lavish disregard of expense; and the said objects washing down huge quantities of "shrimps" and "winkles," with an equal disregard of their own bodily health and subsequent comfort—boys, with great silk hats just balanced on the

op of their heads, smoking cigars, and trying to look as
f they liked them—gentlemen in pink shirts and blue
waistcoats, occasionally upsetting either themselves, or
somebody else, with their own canes.

Some of the finery of these people provokes a smile,
but they are all clean, and happy, and disposed to be
good-natured and sociable. Those two motherly-
looking women in the smart pelisses, who are chatting
so confidentially, inserting a "ma'am" at every fourth
word, scraped an acquaintance about a quarter of an
hour ago: it originated in admiration of the little boy
who belongs to one of them—that diminutive specimen
of mortality in the three-cornered pink satin hat with
black feathers. The two men in the blue coats and drab
trousers, who were walking up and down, smoking their
pipes, are their husbands. The party in the opposite
box are a pretty fair specimen of the generality of the
visitors. These are the father and mother, and old grandmother: a young man and woman, and an individual
addressed by the euphonious title of "Uncle Bill," who
is evidently the wit of the party. They have some half-
dozen children with them, but it is scarcely necessary
to notice the fact, for that is a matter of course here.
Every woman in "the gardens," who has been married
for any length of time, must have had twins on two or
three occasions; it is impossible to account for the
extent of juvenile population in any other way.

Observe the inexpressible delight of the old grandmother, at Uncle Bill's splendid joke of "tea for four:
bread-and-butter for forty"; and the loud explosion of
mirth which follows his wafering a paper "pigtail" on
the waiter's collar. The young man is evidently "keeping
company" with Uncle Bill's niece: and Uncle Bill's
hints—such as "Don't forget me at the dinner, you

know," "I shall look out for the cake, Sally," "I'll be godfather to your first—wager it's a boy," and so forth, are equally embarrassing to the young people, and delightful to the elder ones. As to the old grandmother, she is in perfect ecstasies, and does nothing but laugh herself into fits of coughing, until they have finished the "gin-and-water warm with," of which Uncle Bill ordered "glasses round" after tea, "just to keep the night air out, and do it up comfortable and riglar arter sitch an astonishing hot day!"

It is getting dark, and the people begin to move. The field leading to town is quite full of them; the little hand-chaises are dragged wearily along, the children are tired, and amuse themselves and the company generally by crying, or resort to the much more pleasant expedient of going to sleep—the mothers begin to wish they were at home again—sweethearts grow more sentimental than ever, as the time for parting arrives —the gardens look mournful enough, by the light of the two lanterns which hang against the trees for the convenience of smokers—and the waiters who have been running about incessantly for the last six hours, think they feel a little tired, as they count their glasses and their gains.

A VISIT TO NEWGATE

"The force of habit" is a trite phrase in everybody's mouth; and it is not a little remarkable that those who use it most as applied to others, unconsciously afford in their own persons singular examples of the power which habit and custom exercise over the minds of men, and of the little reflection they are apt to bestow on subjects with which every day's experience has rendered them familiar. If Bedlam could be suddenly removed like another Aladdin's palace, and set down on the space now occupied by Newgate, scarcely one man out of a hundred, whose road to business every morning lies through Newgate Street, or the Old Bailey, would pass the building without bestowing a hasty glance on its small, grated windows, and a transient thought upon the condition of the unhappy beings immured in its dismal cells; and yet these same men, day by day, and hour by hour, pass and repass this gloomy depository of the guilt and misery of London, in one perpetual stream of life and bustle, utterly unmindful of the throng of wretched creatures pent up within it—nay, not even knowing, or if they do, not heeding, the fact that as they pass one particular angle of the massive wall with a light laugh or a merry whistle, they stand within one yard of a fellow-creature, bound and helpless, whose hours are numbered, from whom the last feeble ray of hope has fled for ever, and whose miserable career will shortly terminate in a violent and shameful death. Contact with death even in its least terrible shape is solemn and appalling. How much more awful is it to reflect on this near vicinity to the dying—to men in full health and vigour, in the flower of youth or the prime of life, with all their faculties and perceptions as acute and perfect as your own; but dying, nevertheless—dying as surely—with the hand of death imprinted upon them as indelibly—as if mortal disease had wasted their frames to shadows, and corruption had already begun!

It was with some such thoughts as these that we determined, not many weeks since, to visit the interior of Newgate—in an amateur capacity, of course; and, having carried our intention into effect, we proceed to lay its results before our readers, in the hope—founded more upon the nature of the subject than on any presumptuous confidence in our own descriptive powers—that this paper may not be found wholly devoid of interest. We have only to premise that we do not intend to fatigue the reader with any statistical accounts of the prison; they will be found at length in numerous reports of numerous committees, and a variety of authorities of equal weight. We took no notes, made no memoranda, measured none of the yards, ascertained the exact number of inches in no particular room: are unable even to report of how many apartments the jail is composed.

We saw the prison, and saw the prisoners; and what we did see, and what we thought, we will tell at once in our own way.

Having delivered our credentials to the servant who answered our knock at the door of the governor's house, we were ushered into the "office"; a little room, on the right-hand side as you enter, with two windows looking into the Old Bailey: fitted up like an ordinary attorney's office, or merchant's counting-house, with the usual fixtures—a wainscoted partition, a shelf or two, a desk, a couple of stools, a pair of clerks, an almanack, a clock, and a few maps. After a little delay, occasioned by sending into the interior of the prison for the officer whose duty it was to conduct us, that functionary arrived; a respectable-looking man of about two or three and fifty, in a broad-brimmed hat, and full suit of black, who, but for his keys, would have looked quite as much like a clergyman as a turnkey. We were disappointed; he had not even top-boots on. Following our conductor by a door opposite to that at which we had entered, we arrived at a small room, without any other furniture than a little desk, with a book for visitors' autographs, and a shelf, on which were a few boxes for papers, and casts of the heads and faces of the two notorious murderers, Bishop and Williams; the former, in particular, exhibiting a style of head and set of features, which might have afforded sufficient moral grounds for his instant execution at any time, even had there been no other evidence against him. Leaving this room also, by an opposite door, we found ourself in the lodge which opens on the Old Bailey; one side of which is plentifully garnished with a choice collection of heavy sets of irons, including those worn by the redoubtable Jack Sheppard—genuine; and those *said* to have been graced by the sturdy limbs of the no less celebrated Dick Turpin—doubtful. From this lodge, a heavy oaken gate, bound with iron, studded with nails of the same material, and guarded by another turnkey, opens on a few steps, if we remember right, which terminate in a narrow and dismal stone passage, running parallel with the Old Bailey, and leading to the different yards, through a number of tortuous and intricate windings, guarded in their turn by huge gates and gratings, whose appearance is sufficient to dispel at once the slightest hope of escape that any new-comer may have entertained; and the very recollection of which, on eventually traversing the place again, involves one in a maze of confusion.

It is necessary to explain here that the buildings in the prison, or in other words the different wards—form a square, of which the four sides abut respectively on the Old Bailey, the old College of Physicians (now forming a part of Newgate Market), the Sessions House, and Newgate Street. The intermediate space is divided into several paved yards, in which the prisoners take such air and exercise as can be had in such a place. These yards, with the exception of that in which prisoners under sentence of death are confined (of which we shall presently give a more detailed description), run parallel with Newgate Street, and consequently from the Old Bailey, as it were, to Newgate Market. The women's side is in the right wing of the prison nearest the Sessions House. As we were introduced into this part of the building first, we will adopt the same order, and introduce our readers to it also.

Turning to the right, then, down the passage to which we just now adverted, omitting any mention of intervening gates—for if we noticed every gate that was unlocked for us to pass through, and locked again as soon as we had passed, we should require a gate at every comma—we came to a door composed of thick bars of wood, through which were discernible, passing to and fro in a narrow yard, some twenty women: the majority of whom, however, as soon as they were aware of the presence of strangers, retreated to their wards. One side of this yard is railed off at a considerable distance, and formed into a kind of iron cage, about five feet ten inches in height, roofed at the top, and defended in front by iron bars, from which the friends of the female prisoners communicate with them. In one corner of this singular-looking den was a yellow, haggard, decrepit old woman, in a tattered gown that had once been black, and the remains of an old straw bonnet, with faded ribbon of the same hue, in earnest conversation with a young girl—a prisoner, of course—of about two-and-twenty. It is impossible to imagine a more poverty-stricken object, or a creature so borne down in soul and body, by excess of misery and destitution as the old woman. The girl was a good-looking robust female, with a profusion of hair streaming about in the wind—for she had no bonnet on—and a man's silk pocket-handkerchief loosely thrown over a most ample pair of shoulders. The old woman was talking in that low, stifled tone of voice which tells so forcibly of mental anguish; and every now and then burst into an irrepressible sharp, abrupt cry of grief, the most distressing sound that ears can hear. The girl was perfectly unmoved. Hardened beyond all hope of redemption, she listened doggedly to her mother's entreaties, whatever they were: and, beyond inquiring after "Jem," and eagerly catching at the few halfpence her miserable parent had brought her, took no more apparent interest in the conversation than the most unconcerned spectators. Heaven knows there were enough of them, in the persons of the other prisoners in the yard, who were no more concerned by what was passing before their eyes, and within their hearing, than if they were blind and deaf. Why should they be? Inside the prison, and out, such scenes were too familiar to them to excite even a passing thought, unless of ridicule or contempt for feelings which they had long since forgotten.

A little farther on, a squalid-looking woman in a slovenly, thick-bordered cap, with her arms muffled in a large red shawl, the fringed ends of which straggled nearly to the bottom of a dirty white apron, was communicating some instructions to *her* visitor—her daughter evidently. The girl was thinly clad, and shaking with the cold. Some ordinary word of recognition passed between her and her mother when she appeared at the grating, but neither hope, condolence, regret, nor affection was expressed on either side. The mother whispered her instructions, and the girl received them with her pinched-up half-starved features twisted into an expression of careful cunning. It was some scheme for the woman's defence that she was disclosing, perhaps; and a sullen smile came over the girl's face for an instant, as if she were pleased: not so much at the probability of her mother's liberation, as at the chance of her "getting off" in spite of her prosecutors. The dialogue was soon concluded; and with the same careless indifference with which they had approached each other, the mother turned towards the inner end of the yard, and the girl to the gate at which she had entered.

The girl belonged to a class—unhappily but too extensive—the very existence of which should make men's hearts bleed. Barely past her childhood, it required but a glance to discover that she was one of those children, born and bred in neglect and vice, who have never known what childhood is: who have never been taught to love and court a parent's smile, or to dread a parent's frown. The thousand nameless endearments of childhood, its gaiety and its innocence, are alike unknown to them. They have entered at once upon the stern realities and miseries of life, and to their better nature it is almost hopeless to appeal in after-times, by any of the references which will awaken, if it be only for a moment, some good feeling in ordinary bosoms, however corrupt they may have become. Talk to *them* of parental solicitude, the happy days of childhood, and the merry games of infancy! Tell them of hunger and the streets, beggary and stripes; the gin-shop, the station-house, and the pawnbroker's, and they will understand you.

Two or three women were standing at different parts of the grating, conversing with their friends, but a very large proportion of the prisoners appeared to have no friends at all, beyond such of their old companions as might happen to be within the walls. So, passing hastily down the yard, and pausing only for an instant to notice the little incidents we have just recorded, we were conducted up a clean and well-lighted flight of stone stairs to one of the wards. There are several in this part of the building, but a description of one is a description of the whole.

It was a spacious, bare, whitewashed apartment, lighted of course by windows looking into the interior of the prison, but far more light and airy than one could reasonably expect to find in such a situation. There was a large fire with a deal table before it, round which ten or a dozen women were seated on wooden forms at dinner. Along both sides of the room ran a shelf; below it, at regular intervals, a row of large hooks were fixed in the wall, on each of which was hung the sleeping mat of a prisoner: her rug and blanket being folded up, and placed on the shelf above. At night, these mats are placed on the floor, each beneath the hook on which it hangs during the day; and the ward is thus made to answer the purposes both of a day-room and sleeping apartment. Over the fireplace was a large sheet of pasteboard, on which were displayed a variety of texts from Scripture, which were also scattered about the room in scraps about the size and shape of the copy-slips which are used in schools. On the table was a sufficient provision of a kind of stewed beef and brown bread, in pewter dishes, which are kept perfectly bright, and displayed on shelves in great order and regularity when they are not in use.

The women rose hastily, on our entrance, and retired in a hurried manner to either side of the fireplace. They were all cleanly—many of them decently—attired, and there was nothing peculiar, either in their appearance or demeanour. One or two resumed the needlework which they had probably laid aside at the commence-ment of their meal; others gazed at the visitors with listless curiosity; and a few retired behind their com-panions to the very end of the room, as if desirous to avoid even the casual observation of the strangers. Some old Irishwomen, both in this and other wards, to whom the thing was no novelty, appeared perfectly indifferent to our presence, and remained standing close to the seats from which they had just risen; but the general feeling among the females seemed to be one of uneasiness during the period of our stay among them: which was very brief. Not a word was uttered during the time of our remaining, unless, indeed, by the wardswoman in reply to some question which we put to the turnkey who accompanied us. In every ward on the female side, a wardswoman is appointed to pre-serve order, and a similar regulation is adopted among the males. The wardsmen and wardswomen are all prisoners, selected for good conduct. They alone are allowed the privilege of sleeping on bedsteads; a small stump bedstead being placed in every ward for that purpose. On both sides of the jail is a small receiving-room, to which prisoners are conducted on their first reception, and whence they cannot be removed until they have been examined by the surgeon of the prison.*

Retracing our steps to the dismal passage in which we found ourselves at first (and which, by the bye, contains three or four dark cells for the accommodation of refractory prisoners), we were led through a narrow yard to the "school"—a portion of the prison set apart for boys under fourteen years of age. In a tolerable-sized room, in which were writing-materials and some copy-books, was the schoolmaster, with a couple of his pupils; the remainder having been fetched from an adjoining apartment, the whole were drawn up in line for our inspection. There were fourteen of them in all, some with shoes, some without; some in pinafores without jackets, others in jackets without pinafores, and one in scarce anything at all. The whole number, without an exception we believe, had been committed for trial on charges of pocket-picking; and fourteen such terrible little faces we never beheld. There was not one redeeming feature among them—not a glance of honesty—not a wink expressive of anything but the gallows and the hulks in the whole collection. As to

---

* The regulations of the prison relative to the confinement of prisoners during the day, their sleeping at night, their taking their meals, and other matters of jail economy, have all been altered—greatly for the better—since this sketch was first published. Even the construction of the prison itself has been changed. (Footnote in the "Charles Dickens" Edition.)

anything like shame or contrition, that was entirely out of the question. They were evidently quite gratified at being thought worth the trouble of looking at; their idea appeared to be that we had come to see Newgate as a grand affair, and that they were an indispensable part of the show; and every boy as he "fell in" to the line, actually seemed as pleased and important as if he had done something excessively meritorious in getting there at all. We never looked upon a more disagreeable sight, because we never saw fourteen such hopeless creatures of neglect, before.

On either side of the school-yard is a yard for men, in one of which—that towards Newgate Street— prisoners of the more respectable class are confined. Of the other, we have little description to offer, as the different wards necessarily partake of the same character. They are provided, like the wards on the women's side, with mats and rugs, which are disposed of in the same manner during the day; the only very striking difference between their appearance and that of the wards inhabited by the females is the utter absence of any employment. Huddled together on two opposite forms, by the fireside, sit twenty men perhaps; here, a boy in livery; there, a man in a rough greatcoat and top-boots; farther on, a desperate-looking fellow in his shirtsleeves, with an old Scotch cap upon his shaggy head; near him again, a tall ruffian, in a smock-frock; next to him, a miserable being, of distressed appearance, with his head resting on his hand;—all alike in one respect, all idle and listless. When they do leave the fire, sauntering moodily about, lounging in the window, or leaning against the wall, vacantly swinging their bodies to and fro. With the exception of a man reading an old

A PICKPOCKET IN CUSTODY

newspaper, in two or three instances, this was the case in every ward we entered.

The only communication these men have with their friends is through two close iron gratings, with an intermediate space of about a yard in width between the two, so that nothing can be handed across, nor can the prisoner have any communication by touch with the person who visits him. The married men have a separate grating, at which to see their wives, but its construction is the same.

The prison chapel is situated at the back of the governor's house: the latter having no windows looking into the interior of the prison. Whether the associations connected with the place—the knowledge that here a portion of the burial service is, on some dreadful occasions, performed over the quick and not upon the dead—cast over it a still more gloomy and sombre air than art has imparted to it, we know not, but its appearance is very striking. There is something in a silent and deserted place of worship, solemn and impressive at any time; and the very dissimilarity of this one from any we have been accustomed to only enhances the impression. The meanness of its appointments—the bare and scanty pulpit, with the paltry painted pillars on either side—the women's gallery with its great heavy curtain—the men's with its unpainted benches and dingy front—the tottering little table at the altar, with the Commandments on the wall above it, scarcely legible through lack of paint, and dust and damp—so unlike the velvet and gilding, the marble and wood, of a modern church—are strange and striking. There is one object, too, which rivets the attention and fascinates the gaze, and from which we may turn horror-stricken in vain, for the recollection of it will haunt us, waking and sleeping, for a long time afterwards. Immediately below the reading-desk, on the floor of the chapel, and forming the most conspicuous object in its little area, is *the condemned pew*; a huge black pen, in which the wretched people, who are singled out for death, are placed on the Sunday preceding their execution, in sight of all their fellow-prisoners, from many of whom they may have been separated but a week before, to hear prayers for their own souls, to join in the responses of their own burial service, and to listen to an address, warning their recent companions to take example by their fate, and urging themselves, while there is yet time—nearly four-and-twenty hours—to "turn, and flee from the wrath to come!" Imagine what have been the feelings of the men whom that fearful pew has enclosed, and of whom, between the gallows and the knife, no mortal remnant may now remain! Think of the hopeless clinging to life to the last, and the wild despair, far exceeding in anguish the felon's death itself, by which they have heard the certainty of their speedy transmission to another world, with all their crimes upon their heads, rung into their ears by the officiating clergyman!

At one time—and at no distant period either—the coffins of the men about to be executed were placed in that pew, upon the seat by their side, during the whole service. It may seem incredible, but it is true. Let us hope that the increased spirit of civilisation and humanity which abolished this frightful and degrading custom, may extend itself to other usages equally barbarous; usages which have not even the plea of utility in their defence, as every year's experience has shown them to be more and more inefficacious.

Leaving the chapel, descending to the passage so

frequently alluded to, and crossing the yard before noticed as being allotted to prisoners of a more respectable description than the generality of men confined here, the visitor arrives at a thick iron gate of great size and strength. Having been admitted through it by the turnkey on duty, he turns sharp round to the left, and pauses before another gate; and, having passed this last barrier, he stands in the most terrible part of this gloomy building—the condemned ward.

The press-yard, well known by name to newspaper readers, from its frequent mention in accounts of executions, is at the corner of the building, and next to the ordinary's house, in Newgate Street: running from Newgate Street, towards the centre of the prison, parallel with Newgate Market. It is a long, narrow court, of which a portion of the wall in Newgate Street forms one end, and the gate the other. At the upper end, on the left-hand—that is, adjoining the wall in Newgate Street—is a cistern of water, and at the bottom a double grating (of which the gate itself forms a part) similar to that before described. Through these grates the prisoners are allowed to see their friends; a turnkey always remaining in the vacant space between, during the whole interview. Immediately on the right as you enter is a building containing the press-room, day-room, and cells; the yard is on every side surrounded by lofty walls guarded by *chevaux de frise*; and the whole is under the constant inspection of vigilant and experienced turnkeys.

In the first apartment into which we were con-ducted—which was at the top of a staircase, and immediately over the press-room—were five-and-twenty or thirty prisoners, all under sentence of death, await-ing the result of the recorder's report—men of all ages and appearances, from a hardened old offender with swarthy face and grizzly beard of three days' growth, to a handsome boy, not fourteen years old, and of singularly youthful appearance even for that age, who had been condemned for burglary. There was nothing remarkable in the appearance of these prisoners. One or two decently-dressed men were brooding with a dejected air over the fire; several little groups of two or three had been engaged in conversation at the upper end of the room, or in the windows; and the remainder were crowded round a young man seated at a table, who appeared to be engaged in teaching the younger ones to write. The room was large, airy, and clean. There was very little anxiety or mental suffering depicted in the countenance of any of the men;—they had all been sentenced to death, it is true, and the recorder's report had not yet been made; but, we question whether there was a man among them, notwithstanding, who did not *know* that although he had undergone the ceremony, it never was intended that his life should be sacrificed. On the table lay a Testament, but there were no tokens of its having been in recent use.

In the press-room below were three men, the nature of whose offence rendered it necessary to separate them, even from their companions in guilt. It is a long, sombre room, with two windows sunk into the stone wall, and here the wretched men are pinioned on the morning of their execution, before moving towards the scaffold. The fate of one of these prisoners was uncertain; some mitigatory circumstances having come to light since his trial, which had been humanely represented in the proper quarter. The other two had nothing to expect from the mercy of the Crown; their doom was sealed; no plea could be urged in extenuation of their crime, and they well knew that for them there was no hope in this world. "The two short ones," the turnkey whispered, "were dead men."

The man to whom we have alluded as entertaining some hopes of escape, was lounging, at the greatest distance he could place between himself and his companions, in the window nearest to the door. He was probably aware of our approach, and had assumed an air of courageous indifference; his face was purposely averted towards the window, and he stirred not an inch while we were present. The other two men were at the upper end of the room. One of them, who was imperfectly seen in the dim light, had his back towards us, and was stooping over the fire, with his right arm on the mantelpiece, and his head sunk upon it. The other was leaning on the sill of the farthest window. The light fell full upon him, and communicated to his pale, haggard face, and disordered hair, an appearance which, at that distance, was ghastly. His cheek rested upon his hand; and, with his face a little raised, and his eyes wildly staring before him, he seemed to be unconsciously intent on counting the chinks in the opposite wall. We passed this room again afterwards. The first man was pacing up and down the court with a firm military step—he had been a soldier in the Foot Guards—and a cloth cap jauntily thrown on one side of his head. He bowed respectfully to our conductor, and the salute was returned. The other two still remained in the positions we have described, and were as motionless as statues.[*]

---

[*] These two men were executed shortly afterwards. The other was respited during his Majesty's pleasure. (Footnote in the "Charles Dickens" Edition.)

A few paces up the yard, and forming a continuation of the building, in which are the two rooms we have just quitted, lie the condemned cells. The entrance is by a narrow and obscure staircase leading to a dark passage, in which a charcoal stove casts a lurid tint over the objects in its immediate vicinity, and diffuses something like warmth around. From the left-hand side of this passage, the massive door of every cell on the story opens; and from it alone can they be approached. There are three of these passages, and three of these ranges of cells, one above the other; but in size, furniture and appearance, they are all precisely alike. Prior to the recorder's report being made, all the prisoners under sentence of death are removed from the day-room at five o'clock in the afternoon, and locked up in these cells, where they are allowed a candle until ten o'clock; and here they remain until seven next morning. When the warrant for a prisoner's execution arrives, he is removed to the cells and confined in one of them until he leaves it for the scaffold. He is at liberty to walk in the yard; but, both in his walks and in his cells, he is constantly attended by a turnkey who never leaves him on any pretence.

We entered the first cell. It was a stone dungeon, eight feet long by six wide, with a bench at the upper end, under which were a common rug, a Bible, and prayer-book. An iron candlestick was fixed into the wall at the side; and a small high window in the back admitted as much air and light as could struggle in between a double row of heavy, crossed iron bars. It contained no other furniture of any description.

Conceive the situation of a man, spending his last night on earth in this cell. Buoyed up with some vague and undefined hope of reprieve, he knew not why—

indulging in some wild and visionary idea of escaping, he knew not how—hour after hour of the three preceding days allowed him for preparation has fled with a speed which no man living would deem possible, for none but this dying man can know. He has wearied his friends with entreaties, exhausted the attendants with importunities, neglected in his feverish restlessness the timely warnings of his spiritual consoler; and, now that the illusion is at last dispelled, now that eternity is before him and guilt behind, now that his fears of death amount almost to madness, and an overwhelming sense of his helpless, hopeless state rushes upon him, he is lost and stupefied, and has neither thoughts to turn to, nor power to call upon, the Almighty Being, from whom alone he can seek mercy and forgiveness, and before whom his repentance can alone avail.

Hours have glided by, and still he sits upon the same stone bench with folded arms, heedless alike of the fast decreasing time before him, and the urgent entreaties of the good man at his side. The feeble light is wasting gradually, and the deathlike stillness of the street without, broken only by the rumbling of some passing vehicle which echoes mournfully through the empty yards, warns him that the night is waning fast away. The deep bell of St. Paul's strikes—one! He heard it; it has roused him. Seven hours left! He paces the narrow limits of his cell with rapid strides, cold drops of terror starting on his forehead, and every muscle of his frame quivering with agony. Seven hours! He suffers himself to be led to his seat, mechanically takes the Bible which is placed in his hand, and tries to read and listen. No: his thoughts will wander. The book is torn and soiled by use—and like the book he read his lessons in, at school, just forty years ago! He has never bestowed a thought upon it, perhaps, since he left it as a child: and yet the place, the time, the room—nay, the very boys he played with, crowd as vividly before him as if they were scenes of yesterday; and some forgotten phrase, some childish word, rings in his ears like the echo of one uttered but a minute since. The voice of the clergyman recalls him to himself. He is reading from the sacred book its solemn promises of pardon for repentance, and its awful denunciation of obdurate men. He falls upon his knees and clasps his hands to pray. Hush! what sound was that? He starts upon his feet. It cannot be two yet. Hark! Two quarters have struck; the third—the fourth. It is! Six hours left. Tell him not of repentance! Six hours' repentance for eight times six years of guilt and sin! He buries his face in his hands, and throws himself on the bench.

Worn with watching and excitement, he sleeps, and the same unsettled state of mind pursues him in his dreams. An insupportable load is taken from his breast; he is walking with his wife in a pleasant field, with the bright sky above them, and a fresh and boundless prospect on every side—how different from the stone walls of Newgate! She is looking—not as she did when he saw her for the last time in that dreadful place, but as she used when he loved her—long, long ago, before misery and ill-treatment had altered her looks, and vice had changed his nature, and she is leaning upon his arm, and looking up into his face with tenderness and affection—and he does *not* strike her now, nor rudely shake her from him. And oh! how glad he is to tell her all he had forgotten in that last hurried interview, and to fall on his knees before her and fervently beseech her pardon for all the unkindness and cruelty that wasted her form and broke her heart! The scene suddenly changes. He is on his trial again: there are the judge and jury, and prosecutors, and witnesses, just as they were before. How full the Court is—with a sea of heads—with a gallows, too, and a scaffold—and how all those people stare at *him*! Verdict, "Guilty." No matter; he will escape.

The night is dark and cold, the gates have been left open, and in an instant he is in the street, flying from the scene of this imprisonment like the wind. The streets are cleared, the open fields are gained and the broad wide country lies before him. Onward he dashes in the midst of darkness, over hedge and ditch, through mud and pool, bounding from spot to spot with a speed and lightness astonishing even to himself. At length he pauses; he must be safe from pursuit now; he will stretch himself on that bank and sleep till sunrise.

A period of unconsciousness succeeds. He wakes, cold and wretched. The dull grey light of morning is stealing into the cells, and falls upon the form of the attendant turnkey. Confused by his dreams, he starts from his uneasy bed in momentary uncertainty. It is but momentary. Every object in the narrow cell is too frightfully real to admit of doubt or mistake. He is the condemned felon again, guilty and despairing; and in two hours more will be dead.

THE RIVER

"Are you fond of the water?" is a question very frequently asked, in hot summer weather, by amphibious-looking young men. "Very," is the general reply. "An't you?"—"Hardly ever off it," is the response, accompanied by sundry adjectives, expressive of the speaker's heartfelt admiration of that element. Now, with all respect for the opinion of society in general, and cutter clubs in particular, we humbly suggest that some of the most painful reminiscences in the mind of every individual who has occasionally disported himself on the Thames must be connected with his aquatic recreations. Who ever heard of a successful water-party?—or to put the question in a still more intelligible form, who ever saw one? We have been on water excursions out of number, but we solemnly declare that we cannot call to mind one single occasion of the kind, which was not marked by more miseries than any one would suppose could be reasonably crowded into the space of some eight or nine hours. Something has always gone wrong. Either the cork of the salad-dressing has come out, or the most anxiously expected member of the party has not come out, or the most disagreeable man in company would come out, or a child or two have fallen into the water, or the gentleman who undertook to steer has endangered everybody's life all the way, or the gentlemen who volunteered to row have been "out of practice," and performed very alarming evolutions, putting their oars down into the water and not being able to get them up again, or taking terrific pulls without putting them in at all; in either case, pitching over on the backs of their heads with startling violence, and exhibiting the soles of their pumps to the "sitters" in the boat, in a very humiliating manner.

We grant that the banks of the Thames are very beautiful at Richmond and Twickenham, and other distant havens, often sought though seldom reached; but from the "Red-us" back to Blackfriars Bridge the scene is wonderfully changed. The Penitentiary is a noble building, no doubt, and the sportive youths who "go in" at that particular part of the river, on a summer's evening, may be all very well in perspective; but when you are obliged to keep in shore coming home, and the young ladies will colour up, and look perseveringly the other way, while the married dittoes cough slightly, and stare very hard at the water, you feel awkward—especially if you happen to have been attempting the most distant approach to sentimentality, for an hour or two previously.

Although experience and suffering have produced in our minds the result we have just stated, we are by no means blind to a proper sense of the fun which a looker-on may extract from the amateurs of boating. What can be more amusing than Searle's yard on a fine Sunday morning? It's a Richmond tide, and some dozen boats are preparing for the reception of the parties who have engaged them. Two or three fellows in great rough trousers and Guernsey shirts are getting them ready by easy stages; now coming down the yard with a pair of sculls and a cushion—then having a chat with the "jack," who, like all his tribe, seems to be wholly incapable of doing anything but lounging about—then going back again, and returning with a

46

rudder-line and a stretcher—then solacing themselves with another chat—and then wondering, with their hands in their capacious pockets, "where them gentlemen's got to as ordered the six." One of these, the head man, with the legs of his trousers carefully tucked up at the bottom, to admit the water, we presume—for it is an element in which he is infinitely more at home than on land—is quite a character, and shares with the defunct oyster-swallower the celebrated name of "Dando." Watch him as, taking a few minutes' respite from his toils, he negligently seats himself on the edge of a boat, and fans his broad bushy chest with a cap scarcely half so furry. Look at his magnificent, though reddish whiskers, and mark the somewhat native humour with which he "chaffs" to boys and 'prentices, or cunningly gammons the gen'lm'n into the gift of a glass of gin, of which we verily believe he swallows in one day as much as any six ordinary men, without ever being one atom the worse for it.

But the party arrives, and Dando, relieved from his state of uncertainty, starts up into activity. They approach in full aquatic costume, with round blue jackets, striped shirts, and caps of all sizes and patterns, from the velvet skull-cap of French manufacture to the easy headdress familiar to the students of the old spelling-books, as having, on the authority of the portrait, formed part of the costume of the Reverend Mr. Dilworth.

This is the most amusing time to observe a regular Sunday water-party. There has evidently been up to this period no inconsiderable degree of boasting on everybody's part relative to his knowledge of navigation; the sight of the water rapidly cools their courage, and the air of self-denial with which each of them insists on somebody else's taking an oar, is perfectly delightful.

At length, after a great deal of changing and fidgeting, consequent upon the election of a stroke-oar: the inability of one gentleman to pull on this side, of another to pull on that, and of a third to pull at all, the boat's crew are seated. "Shove her off!" cries the cockswain, who looks as easy and comfortable as if he were steering in the Bay of Biscay. The order is obeyed; the boat is immediately turned completely round, and proceeds towards Westminster Bridge, amidst such a splashing and struggling as never was seen before, except when the *Royal George* went down. "Back wa'ater, sir," shouts Dando, "back wa'ater, you sir, aft"; upon which everybody thinking he must be the individual referred to, they all back water, and back comes the boat, stern first, to the spot whence it started. "Back water, you sir, aft; pull round, you sir, for'ad, can't you?" shouts Dando, in a frenzy of excitement. "Pull round, Tom, can't you?" re-echoes one of the party. "Tom an't for'ad," replies another. "Yes, he is," cries a third; and the unfortunate young man, at the imminent risk of breaking a blood-vessel, pulls and pulls, until the head of the boat fairly lies in the direction of Vauxhall Bridge. "That's right—now pull all on you!" shouts Dando again, adding, in an undertone, to somebody by him, "Blowed if hever I see sich a set of muffs!" and away jogs the boat in a zigzag direction, every one of the six oars dipping into the water at a different time; and the yard is once more clear, until the arrival of the next party.

A well-contested rowing-match on the Thames is a very lively and interesting scene. The water is studded with boats of all sorts, kinds, and descriptions; places in the coal-barges at the different wharfs are let to crowds of spectators, beer and tobacco flow freely about; men, women, and children wait for the start in breathless expectation; cutters of six and eight oars glide gently up and down, waiting to accompany their *protégés* during the race; bands of music add to the animation, if not to the harmony of the scene; groups of watermen are assembled at the different stairs, discussing the merits of the respective candidates; and the prize wherry, which is rowed slowly about by a pair of sculls, is an object of general interest.

Two o'clock strikes, and everybody looks anxiously in the direction of the bridge through which the candidates for the prize will come—half-past two, and the general attention which has been preserved so long begins to flag, when suddenly a gun is heard, and a noise of distant hurra'ing along each bank of the river—every head is bent forward—the noise draws nearer and nearer—the boats which have been waiting at the bridge start briskly up the river, and a well-manned galley shoots through the arch, the sitters cheering on the boats behind them, which are not yet visible.

"Here they are," is the general cry—and through darts the first boat, the men in her stripped to the skin, and exerting every muscle to preserve the advantage they have gained—four other boats follow close astern; there are not two boats' length between them—the shouting is tremendous, and the interest intense. "Go on, Pink"—"Give it her, Red"—"Sulliwin for ever"—"Bravo! George"—"Now, Tom, now—now—now—why don't your partner stretch out?"—"Two pots to a pint on Yellow," &c., &c. Every little public-house fires its gun, and hoists its flag; and the men who win the heat come in, amidst a splashing and shouting, and banging and confusion, which no one can imagine who has not witnessed it, and of which any description would convey a very faint idea.

One of the most amusing places we know is the steam-wharf of the London Bridge, or St. Katharine's Dock Company, on a Saturday morning in summer, when the Gravesend and Margate steamers are usually crowded to excess; and as we have just taken a glance at the river above bridge, we hope our readers will not object to accompany us on board a Gravesend packet.

Coaches are every moment setting down at the entrance to the wharf, and the stare of bewildered astonishment with which the "fares" resign themselves and their luggage into the hands of the porters, who seize all the packages at once as a matter of course, and run away with them, Heaven knows where, is laughable in the extreme. A Margate boat lies alongside the wharf, the Gravesend boat (which starts first) lies alongside that again; and as a temporary communication is formed between the two, by means of a plank and hand-rail, the natural confusion of the scene is by no means diminished.

"Gravesend?" inquires a stout father of a stout family, who follow him, under the guidance of their mother, and a servant, at the no small risk of two or three of them being left behind in the confusion. "Gravesend?"

"Pass on, if you please, sir," replies the attendant—"other boat, sir."

Hereupon the stout father, being rather mystified, and the stout mother rather distracted by maternal anxiety, the whole party deposit themselves in the Margate boat, and after having congratulated himself on having secured very comfortable seats, the stout father sallies to the chimney to look for his luggage,

STEAM EXCURSION

which he has a faint recollection of having given some man something, to take somewhere. No luggage, however, bearing the most remote resemblance to his own, in shape or form, is to be discovered; on which the stout father calls very loudly for an officer, to whom he states the case, in the presence of another father of another family—a little thin man—who entirely concurs with him (the stout father) in thinking that it's high time something was done with these steam companies, and that as the Corporation Bill failed to do it, something else must; for really people's property is not to be sacrificed in this way; and that if the luggage isn't restored without delay, he will take care it shall be put in the papers, for the public is not to be the victim of these great monopolies. To this, the officer, in his turn, replies, that that company, ever since it has been St. Kat'rine's Dock Company, has protected life and property; that if it had been the London Bridge Wharf Company, indeed, he shouldn't have wondered, seeing that the morality of that company (they being the opposition) can't be answered for, by no one; but as it is, he's convinced there must be some mistake, and he wouldn't mind making a solemn oath afore a magistrate that the gentleman'll find his luggage afore he gets to Margate.

Here the stout father, thinking he is making a capital point, replies, that as it happens, he is not going to Margate at all, and that "Passenger to Gravesend" was on the luggage, in letters of full two inches long; on which the officer rapidly explains the mistake, and the stout mother, and the stout children, and the servant, are hurried with all possible despatch on board the Gravesend boat, which they reach just in time to discover that their luggage is there, and that their comfortable seats are not. Then the bell, which is the signal for the Gravesend boat starting, begins to ring most furiously: and people keep time to the bell, by running in and out of our boat at a double-quick pace. The bell stops; the boat starts: people who have been taking leave of their friends on board are carried away against their will; and people who have been taking leave of their friends on shore find that they have performed a very needless ceremony, in consequence of their not being carried away at all. The regular passengers, who have season tickets, go below to breakfast; people who have purchased morning papers compose themselves to read them; and people who have not been down the river before think that both the shipping and the water look a great deal better at a distance.

When we get down about as far as Blackwall, and begin to move at a quicker rate, the spirits of the passengers appear to rise in proportion. Old women who have brought large wicker hand-baskets with them set seriously to work at the demolition of heavy sandwiches, and pass round a wine-glass, which is frequently replenished from a flat bottle like a stomach-warmer, with considerable glee: handing it first to the gentleman in the forage-cap, who plays the harp—partly as an expression of satisfaction with his previous exertions; and partly to induce him to play "Dumbledumb-deary," for "Alick" to dance to; which being done, Alick, who is a damp earthy child in red worsted socks, takes certain small jumps upon the deck, to the unspeakable satisfaction of his family circle. Girls who have brought the first volume of some new novel in their reticule become extremely plaintive, and expatiate to Mr. Brown, or young Mr. O'Brien, who has been looking over them, on the blueness of the sky, and brightness of the water; on which Mr. Brown or Mr. O'Brien, as the case may be, remarks in a low voice that he has been quite insensible of late to the beauties of nature—that his whole thoughts and wishes have centred in one object alone—whereupon the young lady looks up, and failing in her attempt to appear unconscious, looks down again; and turns over the next leaf with great difficulty, in order to afford opportunity for a lengthened pressure of the hand.

Telescopes, sandwiches, and glasses of brandy-and-water cold without, begin to be in great requisition; and bashful men who have been looking down the hatchway at the engine find, to their great relief, a subject on which they can converse with one another—and a copious one too—Steam.

"Wonderful thing steam, sir." "Ah! (a deep-drawn sigh) it is indeed, sir." "Great power, sir." "Immense—immense!" "Great deal done by steam, sir." "Ah! (another sigh at the immensity of the subject, and a knowing shake of the head) you may say that, sir." "Still in its infancy, they say, sir." Novel remarks of this kind, are generally the commencement of a conversation which is prolonged until the conclusion of the trip, and, perhaps, lays the foundation of a speaking acquaintance between half-a-dozen gentlemen, who, having their families at Gravesend, take season tickets for the boat, and dine on board regularly every afternoon.

MEDITATIONS IN MONMOUTH STREET

We have always entertained a particular attachment towards Monmouth Street, as the only true and real emporium for second-hand wearing apparel. Monmouth Street is venerable from its antiquity, and respectable from its usefulness. Holywell Street we despise; the red-headed and red-whiskered Jews who forcibly haul you into their squalid houses, and thrust you into a suit of clothes, whether you will or not, we detest.

The inhabitants of Monmouth Street are a distinct class; a peaceable and retiring race, who immure themselves for the most part in deep cellars, or small back-parlours, and who seldom come forth into the world, except in the dusk and coolness of the evening, when they may be seen seated, in chairs on the pavement, smoking their pipes, or watching the gambols of their engaging children as they revel in the gutter, a happy troop of infantine scavengers. Their countenances bear a thoughtful and a dirty cast, certain indications of their love of traffic; and their habitations are distinguished by that disregard of outward appearance and neglect of personal comfort, so common among people who are constantly immersed in profound speculations, and deeply engaged in sedentary pursuits.

We have hinted at the antiquity of our favourite spot. "A Monmouth Street laced coat" was a by-word a century ago; and still we find Monmouth Street the same. Pilot greatcoats with wooden buttons have usurped the place of the ponderous laced coats with full skirts; embroidered waistcoats with large flaps have yielded to double-breasted checks with roll-collars; and three-cornered hats of quaint appearance have given place to the low crowns and broad brims of the coachman school; but it is the times that have changed, not Monmouth Street. Through every alteration and every change, Monmouth Street has still remained the burial-place of the fashions; and such, to judge from all present appearances, it will remain until there are no more fashions to bury.

We love to walk among these extensive groves of the illustrious dead, and to indulge in the speculations to which they give rise; now fitting a deceased coat, then a dead pair of trousers, and anon the mortal remains of a gaudy waistcoat, upon some being of our own conjuring up, and endeavouring, from the shape and fashion of the garment itself, to bring its former owner before our mind's eye. We have gone on speculating in this way, until whole rows of coats have started from their pegs, and buttoned up, of their own accord, round the waists of imaginary wearers; lines of trousers have jumped down to meet them; waistcoats have almost burst with anxiety to put themselves on; and half an acre of shoes have suddenly found feet to fit them, and gone stumping down the street with a noise which has fairly awakened us from our pleasant reverie, and driven us slowly away, with a bewildered stare, an object of astonishment to the good people of Monmouth Street, and of no slight suspicion to the policeman at the opposite street-corner.

We were occupied in this manner the other day, endeavouring to fit a pair of lace-up half-boots on an ideal personage, for whom, to say the truth, they were full a couple of sizes too small, when our eyes happened to alight on a few suits of clothes ranged outside a shop-window, which it immediately struck us must at different periods have all belonged to, and been worn by, the same individual, and had now, by one of those strange conjunctions of circumstances which will occur sometimes, come to be exposed together for sale in the same shop. The idea seemed a fantastic one, and we looked at the clothes again with a firm determination not to be easily led away. No, we were right; the more we looked, the more we were convinced of the accuracy of our previous impression. There was the man's whole life written as legibly on those clothes, as if we had his autobiography engrossed on parchment before us.

The first was a patched and much-soiled skeleton suit; one of those straight blue cloth cases in which small boys used to be confined, before belts and tunics had come in, and old notions had gone out: an ingenious contrivance for displaying the full symmetry of a boy's figure, by fastening him into a very tight jacket, with an ornamental row of buttons over each shoulder, and then buttoning his trousers over it, so as to give his legs the appearance of being hooked on, just under the armpits. This was the boy's dress. It had belonged to a town boy, we could see; there was a shortness about the legs and arms of the suit; and a bagging at the knees, peculiar to the rising youth of London streets. A small day-school he had been at, evidently. If it had been a regular boys' school they wouldn't have let him play on the floor so much, and rub his knees so white. He had an indulgent mother too, and plenty of halfpence, as the numerous smears of some sticky substance about the pockets, and just below the chin, which even the salesman's skill could not succeed in disguising, sufficiently betokened. They were decent people, but not overburdened with riches, or he would not have so far outgrown the suit when he passed into those corduroys with the round jacket; in which he went to a boys' school, however, and learnt to write—and in ink of pretty tolerable blackness, too, if the place where he used to wipe his pen might be taken as evidence.

A black suit and the jacket changed into a diminutive coat. His father had died, and the mother had got the boy a message-lad's place in some office. A long-worn suit that one; rusty and threadbare before it was laid aside, but clean and free from soil to the last. Poor woman! We could imagine her assumed cheerfulness over the scanty meal, and the refusal of her own small portion, that her hungry boy might have enough. Her constant anxiety for his welfare, her pride in his growth mingled sometimes with the thought, almost too acute to bear, that as he grew to be a man his old affection might cool, old kindnesses fade from his mind, and old promises be forgotten—the sharp pain that even then a careless word or a cold look would give her—all crowded on our thoughts as vividly as if the very scene were passing before us.

These things happen every hour, and we all know it; and yet we felt as much sorrow when we saw, or fancied we saw—it makes no difference which—the change that began to take place now, as if we had just conceived the bare possibility of such a thing for the first time. The next suit, smart but slovenly; meant to be gay, and yet not half so decent as the threadbare apparel; redolent of the idle lounge, and the blackguard companions, told us, we thought, that the widow's comfort had rapidly faded away. We could imagine that coat—imagine! we could see it; we *had* seen it a hundred times—sauntering in company with three or four other coats of the same cut, about some place of profligate resort at night.

MONMOUTH STREET

We dressed, from the same shop-window in an instant, half-a-dozen boys of from fifteen to twenty; and putting cigars into their mouths, and their hands into their pockets, watched them as they sauntered down the street, and lingered at the corner, with the obscene jest, and the oft-repeated oath. We never lost sight of them, till they had cocked their hats a little more on one side, and swaggered into the public-house; and then we entered the desolate home, where the mother sat late in the night, alone; we watched her, as she paced the room in feverish anxiety, and every now and then opened the door, looked wistfully into the dark and empty street, and again returned, to be again and again disappointed. We beheld the look of patience with which she bore the brutish threat, nay, even the drunken blow; and we heard the agony of tears that gushed from her very heart, as she sank upon her knees in her solitary and wretched apartment.

A long period had elapsed, and a greater change had taken place, by the time of casting off the suit that hung above. It was that of a stout, broad-shouldered, sturdy-chested man; and we knew at once, as anybody would, who glanced at that broad-skirted green coat, with the large metal buttons, that its wearer seldom walked forth without a dog at his heels, and some idle ruffian, the very counterpart of himself, at his side. The vices of the boy had grown with the man, and we fancied his home then—if such a place deserve the name.

We saw the bare and miserable room, destitute of furniture, crowded with his wife and children, pale, hungry, and emaciated; the man cursing their lamentations, staggering to the tap-room, from whence he had just returned, followed by his wife and a sickly infant, clamouring for bread; and heard the street-wrangle and noisy recrimination that his striking her occasioned. And then imagination led us to some metropolitan workhouse, situated in the midst of crowded streets and alleys, filled with noxious vapours, and ringing with boisterous cries, where an old and feeble woman, imploring pardon for her son, lay dying in a close dark room, with no child to clasp her hand, and no pure air from heaven to fan her brow. A stranger closed the eyes that settled into a cold unmeaning glare, and strange ears received the words that murmured from the white and half-closed lips.

A coarse round frock, with a worn cotton neckerchief, and other articles of clothing of the commonest description, completed the history. A prison, and the sentence—banishment or the gallows. What would the man have given then, to be once again the contented humble drudge of his boyish years; to have restored to life, but for a week, a day, an hour, a minute, only for so long a time as would enable him to say one word of passionate regret to, and hear one sound of heartfelt forgiveness from, the cold and ghastly form that lay rotting in the pauper's grave! The children wild in the streets, the mother a destitute widow; both deeply tainted with the deep disgrace of the husband and father's name, and impelled by sheer necessity down the precipice that had led him to a lingering death, possibly of many years' duration, thousands of miles away. We had no clue to the end of the tale; but it was easy to guess its termination.

We took a step or two further on, and by way of restoring the naturally cheerful tone of our thoughts, began fitting visionary feet and legs into a cellar-board full of boots and shoes, with a speed and accuracy that would have astonished the most expert artist in leather, living. There was one pair of boots in particular—a jolly, good-tempered, hearty-looking pair of tops, that excited our warmest regard; and we had got a fine, red-faced, jovial fellow of a market-gardener into them, before we had made their acquaintance half a minute. They were just the very thing for him. There were his huge fat legs bulging over the tops, and fitting them too tight to admit of his tucking in the loops he had pulled them on by; and his knee-cords with an interval of stocking; and his blue apron tucked up round his waist; and his red neckerchief and blue coat, and a white hat stuck on one side of his head; and there he stood with a broad grin on his great red face, whistling away, as if any other idea but that of being happy and comfortable had never entered his brain.

This was the very man after our own heart; we knew all about him; we had seen him coming up to Covent Garden in his green chaise-cart, with the fat tubby little horse, half a thousand times; and even while we cast an affectionate look upon his boots, at that instant, the form of a coquettish servant-maid suddenly sprung into a pair of Denmark satin shoes that stood beside them, and we at once recognised the very girl who accepted his offer of a ride, just on this side of the Hammersmith Suspension Bridge, the very last Tuesday morning we rode into town from Richmond.

A very smart female, in a showy bonnet, stepped into a pair of grey cloth boots, with black fringe and binding, that were studiously pointing out their toes on the other side of the top-boots, and seemed very anxious to engage his attention, but we didn't observe that our friend the market-gardener appeared at all captivated with these blandishments; for beyond giving a knowing wink when they first began, as if to imply that he quite understood their end and object, he took no further notice of them. His indifference, however, was amply recompensed by the excessive gallantry of a very old gentleman with a silver-headed stick, who tottered into a pair of large list shoes, that were standing in one corner of the board, and indulged in a variety of gestures expressive of his admiration of the lady in the cloth boots, to the immeasurable amusement of a young fellow we put into a pair of long-quartered pumps, who we thought would have split the coat that slid down to meet him, with laughing.

We had been looking on at this little pantomime with great satisfaction for some time, when, to our unspeakable astonishment, we perceived that the whole of the characters, including a numerous *corps de ballet* of boots and shoes in the background, into which we had been hastily thrusting as many feet as we could press into the service, were arranging themselves in order for dancing; and some music striking up at the moment, to it they went without delay. It was perfectly delightful to witness the agility of the market-gardener. Out went the boots, first on one side, then on the other, then cutting, then shuffling, then setting to the Denmark satins, then advancing, then retreating, then going round, and then repeating the whole of the evolutions again, without appearing to suffer in the least from the violence of the exercise.

Nor were the Denmark satins a bit behindhand, for they jumped and bounded about, in all directions; and though they were neither so regular, nor so true to the time as the cloth boots, still, as they seemed to do it from the heart, and to enjoy it more, we candidly confess that we preferred their style of dancing to the other. But the old gentleman in the list shoes was the most amusing object in the whole party; for, besides his grotesque attempts to appear youthful, and amorous, which were sufficiently entertaining in themselves, the young fellow in the pumps managed so artfully that every time the old gentleman advanced to salute the lady in the cloth boots, he trod with his whole weight on the old fellow's toes, which made him roar with anguish, and rendered all the others like to die of laughing.

We were in the full enjoyment of these festivities when we heard a shrill, and by no means musical voice, exclaim, "Hope you'll know me agin, imperence!" and on looking intently forward to see from whence the sound came, we found that it proceeded, not from the young lady in the cloth boots, as we had at first been inclined to suppose, but from a bulky lady of elderly appearance who was seated in a chair at the head of the cellar-steps, apparently for the purpose of superintending the sale of the articles arranged there.

A barrel-organ, which had been in full force close behind us, ceased playing; the people we had been fitting into the shoes and boots took to flight at the interruption; and as we were conscious that in the depth of our meditations we might have been rudely staring at the old lady for half an hour without knowing it, we took to flight too, and were soon immersed in the deepest obscurity of the adjacent "Dials."

THE FIRST OF MAY

"Now ladies, up in the sky-parlour: only once a
year, if you please!"

YOUNG LADY WITH BRASS LADLE

"Sweep—sweep—sw-e-ep!"

ILLEGAL WATCHWORD

The first of May! There is a merry freshness in the
sound, calling to our minds a thousand thoughts of all
that is pleasant in nature and beautiful in her most
delightful form. What man is there, over whose mind a
bright spring morning does not exercise a magic
influence—carrying him back to the days of his childish
sports, and conjuring up before him the old green field
with its gently-waving trees, where the birds sang as
he has never heard them since—where the butterfly
fluttered far more gaily than he ever sees him now,
in all his ramblings—where the sky seemed bluer,
and the sun shone more brightly—where the air blew
more freshly over greener grass, and sweeter-smelling
flowers—where everything wore a richer and more
brilliant hue than it is ever dressed in now! Such are the
deep feelings of childhood, and such are the impressions
which every lovely object stamps upon its heart! The
hardy traveller wanders through the maze of thick and
pathless woods, where the sun's rays never shone, and
heaven's pure air never played; he stands on the brink
of the roaring waterfall, and, giddy and bewildered,

watches the foaming mass as it leaps from stone to stone, and from crag to crag; he lingers in the fertile plains of a land of perpetual sunshine, and revels in the luxury of their balmy breath. But what are the deep forests, or the thundering waters, or the richest land-scapes that bounteous nature ever spread, to charm the eyes, and captivate the senses of man, compared with the recollection of the old scenes of his early youth? Magic scenes indeed; for the fancies of childhood dressed them in colours brighter than the rainbow, and almost as fleeting!

In former times, spring brought with it not only such associations as these, connected with the past, but sports and games for the present—merry dances round rustic pillars, adorned with emblems of the season, and reared in honour of its coming. Where are they now? Pillars we have, but they are no longer rustic ones; and as to dancers, they are used to rooms, and light, and would not show well in the open air. Think of the immorality, too! What would your sabbath enthusiasts say to an aristocratic ring encircling the Duke of York's Column in Carlton Terrace—a grand *poussette* of the middle classes, round Alderman Waithman's monument in Fleet Street—or a general hands-four-round of ten-pound householders, at the foot of the Obelisk in St. George's Fields? Alas! romance can make no head against the Riot Act; and pastoral simplicity is not understood by the police.

Well; many years ago we began to be a steady and matter-of-fact sort of people, and dancing in spring being beneath our dignity, we gave it up, and in course of time it descended to the sweeps—a fall certainly, because, though sweeps are very good fellows in their way, and moreover very useful in a civilised community, they are not exactly the sort of people to give the tone to the little elegances of society. The sweeps, however, got the dancing to themselves, and they kept it up, and handed it down. This was a severe blow to the romance of springtime, but it did not entirely destroy it, either; for a portion of it descended to the sweeps with the dancing, and rendered them objects of great interest. A mystery hung over the sweeps in those days. Legends were in existence of wealthy gentlemen who had lost children, and who, after many years of sorrow and suffering, had found them in the character of sweeps. Stories were related of a young boy who, having been stolen from his parents in his infancy, and devoted to the occupation of chimney-sweeping, was sent, in the course of his professional career, to sweep the chimney of his mother's bedroom; and how, being hot and tired when he came out of the chimney, he got into the bed he had so often slept in as an infant, and was discovered and recognised therein by his mother, who once every year of her life, thereafter, requested the pleasure of the company of every London sweep, at half-past one o'clock, to roast beef, plum-pudding, porter, and six-pence.

Such stories as these, and there were many such, threw an air of mystery round the sweeps, and produced for them some of those good effects which animals derive from the doctrine of the transmigration of souls. No one (except the masters) thought of ill-treating a sweep, because no one knew who he might be, or what nobleman's or gentleman's son he might turn out. Chimney-sweeping was, by many believers in the marvellous, considered as a sort of probationary term, at an earlier or later period of which divers young noblemen were to come into possession of their rank and titles: and the profession was held by them in great respect accordingly.

We remember, in our young days, a little sweep about our own age, with curly hair and white teeth, whom we devoutly and sincerely believed to be the lost son and heir of some illustrious personage—an impression which was resolved into an unchangeable conviction on our infant mind, by the subject of our speculations informing us, one day, in reply to our question, propounded a few moments before his ascent to the summit of the kitchen chimney, "that he believed he'd been born in the vurkis, but he'd never know'd his father." We felt certain, from that time forth, that he would one day be owned by a lord; and we never heard the church-bells ring, or saw a flag hoisted in the neighbourhood, without thinking that the happy event had at last occurred, and that his long-lost parent had arrived in a coach and six, to take him home to Grosvenor Square. He never came, however; and, at the present moment, the young gentleman in question is settled down as a master sweep in the neighbourhood of Battle Bridge, his distinguishing characteristics being a decided antipathy to washing himself, and the possession of a pair of legs very inadequate to the support of his unwieldy and corpulent body.

The romance of spring having gone out before our time, we were fain to console ourselves as we best could with the uncertainty that enveloped the birth and parentage of its attendant dancers, the sweeps; and we *did* console ourselves with it, for many years. But, even this wretched source of comfort received a shock from which it has never recovered—a shock which has been in reality its death-blow. We could not disguise from ourselves the fact that whole families of sweeps were regularly born of sweeps, in the rural districts of Somers Town and Camden Town—that the eldest son succeeded to the father's business, that the other branches assisted him therein, and commenced on their own account; that their children again were educated to the profession; and that about their identity there could be no mistake whatever. We could not be blind, we say, to this melancholy truth, but we could not bring ourselves to admit it, nevertheless, and we lived on for some years in a state of voluntary ignorance. We were roused from our pleasant slumber by certain dark insinuations thrown out by a friend of ours, to the effect that children in the lower ranks of life were beginning to *choose* chimney-sweeping as their particular walk; that applications had been made by various boys to the constituted authorities, to allow them to pursue the object of their ambition with the full concurrence and sanction of the law; that the affair, in short, was becoming one of mere legal contract. We turned a deaf ear to these rumours at first, but slowly and surely they stole upon us. Month after month, week after week, nay, day after day, at last, did we meet with accounts of similar applications. The veil was removed, all mystery was at an end, and chimney-sweeping had become a favourite and chosen pursuit. There is no longer any occasion to steal boys; for boys flock in crowds to bind themselves. The romance of the trade has fled, and the chimney-sweeper of the present day is no more like unto him of thirty years ago than is a Fleet Street pickpocket to a Spanish brigand, or Paul Pry to Caleb Williams.

This gradual decay and disuse of the practice of leading noble youths into captivity, and compelling them to ascend chimneys, was a severe blow, if we may so speak, to the romance of chimney-sweeping, and to the romance of spring at the same time. But even this was not all, for some few years ago the dancing on May Day began to decline; small sweeps were observed to congregate in twos or threes, unsupported by a "green," with no "My Lord" to act as master of the ceremonies, and no "My Lady" to preside over the exchequer. Even in companies where there was a "green" it was an absolute nothing—a mere sprout—and the instrumental accompaniments rarely extended beyond the shovels and a set of Pan's pipes, better known to the many as a "mouth-organ."

These were signs of the times, portentous omens of a coming change; and what was the result which they shadowed forth? Why, the master sweeps, influenced by a restless spirit of innovation, actually interposed their authority, in opposition to the dancing, and substituted a dinner—an anniversary dinner at White Conduit House—where clean faces appeared in lieu of black ones smeared with rose pink; and knee cords and tops superseded nankeen drawers and rosetted shoes.

Gentlemen who were in the habit of riding shy horses; and steady-going people who have no vagrancy in their souls, lauded this alteration to the skies, and the conduct of the master sweeps was described as beyond the reach of praise. But how stands the real fact? Let any man deny, if he can, that when the cloth had been removed, fresh pots and pipes laid upon the table, and the customary loyal and patriotic toasts proposed, the celebrated Mr. Sluffen, of Adam and Eve Court, whose authority not the most malignant of our opponents can call in question, expressed himself in a manner following: "That now he'd cotcht the cheerman's hi, he vished he might be jolly veil blessed, if he won't a-goin' to have his innings, vich he vould say these here obserwashuns—that how some mischeevus coves as know'd nuffin about the consarn, had tried to sit people agin the mas'r swips, and take the shine out o' their bis'nes, and the bread out o' the traps o' their preshus kids, by a-makin' o' this here remark, as chimblies could be as vell svept by 'sheenery as by boys; and that the makin' use o' boys for that there purpuss vos barbareous; vereas, he 'ad been a chummy—he begged the cheerman's parding for usin' such a wulgar hexpression—more nor thirty year—he might say he'd been born in a chimbley—and he know'd uncommon veil as 'sheenery vos vus nor o' no use: and as to kerhewelty to the boys, everybody in the chimbley line know'd as veil as he did, that they liked the climbin' better nor nuffin as vos." From this day, we date the total fall of the last lingering remnant of May Day dancing, among the *élite* of the profession: and from this period we commence a new era in that portion of our spring associations which relates to the 1st of May.

We are aware that the unthinking part of the population will meet us here, with the assertion that dancing on May Day still continues—that "greens" are annually seen to roll along the streets—that youths in the garb of clowns precede them, giving vent to the ebullitions of their sportive fancies; and that lords and ladies follow in their wake.

Granted. We are ready to acknowledge that in outward show these processions have greatly improved: we do not deny the introduction of solos on the drum; we will even go so far as to admit an occasional fantasia on the triangle, but here our admissions end. We positively deny that the sweeps have art or part in these proceedings. We distinctly charge the dustmen with throwing what they ought to clear away, into the eyes of the public. We accuse scavengers, brickmakers, and gentlemen who devote their energies to the coster-mongering line, with obtaining money once a year, under false pretences. We cling with peculiar fondness to the custom of days gone by, and have shut out conviction as long as we could, but it has forced itself upon us; and we now proclaim to a deluded public that the May Day dancers are *not* sweeps. The size of them, alone, is sufficient to repudiate the idea. It is a notorious fact, that the widely-spread taste for register-stoves has materially increased the demand for small boys; whereas the men, who, under a fictitious character, dance about the streets on the first of May nowadays, would be a tight fit in a kitchen flue, to say nothing of the parlour. This is strong presumptive evidence, but we have positive proof—the evidence of our own senses. And here is our testimony.

Upon the morning of the second of the merry month of May, in the year of our Lord one thousand eight hundred and thirty-six, we went out for a stroll, with a kind of forlorn hope of seeing something or other which might induce us to believe that it was really spring, and not Christmas. After wandering as far as Copenhagen House, without meeting anything calculated to dispel our impression that there was a mistake in the alman-acks, we turned back down Maiden Lane, with the intention of passing through the extensive colony lying between it and Battle Bridge, which is inhabited by pro-prietors of donkey-carts, boilers of horse-flesh, makers of tiles, and sifters of cinders; through which colony we should have passed, without stoppage or interruption, if a little crowd gathered round a shed had not attracted our attention, and induced us to pause.

When we say a "shed," we do not mean the conservatory sort of building, which, according to the old song, Love tenanted when he was a young man, but a wooden house with windows stuffed with rags and paper, and a small yard at the side with one dust-cart, two baskets, a few shovels, and little heaps of cinders, and fragments of china and tiles, scattered about it. Before this inviting spot we paused; and the longer we looked, the more we wondered what exciting circumstance it could be that induced the foremost members of the crowd to flatten their noses against the parlour window, in the vain hope of catching a glimpse of what was going on inside. After staring vacantly about us for some minutes, we appealed, touching the cause of this assemblage, to a gentleman in a suit of tarpauling, who was smoking his pipe on our right hand; but as the only answer we obtained was a playful inquiry whether our mother had disposed of her mangle, we determined to wait the issue in silence.

Judge of our virtuous indignation, when the street-door of the shed opened, and a party emerged therefrom, clad in the costume and emulating the appearance of May Day sweeps!

The first person who appeared was "my lord," habited in a blue coat and bright buttons, with gilt paper tacked over the seams, yellow knee-breeches, pink cotton stockings, and shoes; a cocked hat, ornamented with shreds of various-coloured paper, on his head, a *bouquet*, the size of a prize cauliflower, in his button-hole, a long Belcher handkerchief in his right hand, and a thin cane in his left. A murmur of applause ran through the crowd (which was chiefly composed of his lordship's personal friends), when this graceful figure made his appearance, which swelled into a burst of

George Cruikshank

THE FIRST OF MAY

applause as his fair partner in the dance bounded forth to join him. Her ladyship was attired in pink crape over bed-furniture, with a low body and short sleeves. The symmetry of her ankles was partially concealed by a very perceptible pair of frilled trousers; and the inconvenience which might have resulted from the circumstance of her white satin shoes being a few sizes too large was obviated by their being firmly attached to her legs with strong tape sandals.

Her head was ornamented with a profusion of artificial flowers; and in her hand she bore a large brass ladle, wherein to receive what she figuratively denominated "the tin." The other characters were a young gentleman in girl's clothes and a widow's cap; two clowns who walked upon their hands in the mud, to the immeasurable delight of all the spectators; a man with a drum; another man with a flageolet; a dirty woman in a large shawl, with a box under her arm for the money—and last, though not least, the "green," animated by no less a personage than our identical friend, in the tarpauling suit.

The man hammered away at the drum, the flageolet squeaked, the shovels rattled, the "green" rolled about, pitching first on one side and then on the other; my lady threw her right foot over her left ankle, and her left foot over her right ankle, alternately; my lord ran a few paces forward, and butted at the "green," and then a few paces backward upon the toes of the crowd, and then went to the right, and then to the left, and then dodged my lady round the "green"; and finally drew her arm through his, and called upon the boys to shout, which they did lustily—for this was the dancing.

We passed the same group, accidentally, in the evening. We never saw a "green" so drunk, a lord so quarrelsome (no: not even in the House of Peers after dinner), a pair of clowns so melancholy, a lady so muddy, or a party so miserable.

How has May Day decayed!

Gin-Shops

It is a remarkable circumstance that different trades appear to partake of the disease to which elephants and dogs are especially liable, and to run stark, staring, raving mad, periodically. The great distinction between the animals and the trades is that the former run mad with a certain degree of propriety—they are very regular in their irregularities. We know the period at which the emergency will arise, and provide against it accordingly. If an elephant run mad, we are all ready for him—kill or cure—pills or bullets, calomel in conserve of roses, or lead in a musket-barrel. If a dog happen to look unpleasantly warm in the summer months, and to trot about the shady side of the streets with a quarter of a yard of tongue hanging out of his mouth, a thick leather muzzle, which has been previously prepared in compliance with the thoughtful injunctions of the Legislature, is instantly clapped over his head, by way of making him cooler, and he either looks remarkably unhappy for the next six weeks, or becomes legally insane, and goes mad, as it were, by Act of Parliament. But these trades are as eccentric as comets; nay, worse, for no one can calculate on the recurrence of the strange appearances which betoken the disease. Moreover, the contagion is general, and the quickness with which it diffuses itself almost incredible.

We will cite two or three cases in illustration of our meaning. Six or eight years ago, the epidemic began to display itself among the linendrapers and haberdashers.

The primary symptoms were an inordinate love of plate-glass, and a passion for gas-lights and gilding. The disease gradually progressed, and at last attained a fearful height. Quiet dusty old shops in different parts of town were pulled down; spacious premises with stuccoed fronts and gold letters were erected instead; floors were covered with Turkey carpets; roofs supported by massive pillars; doors knocked into windows; a dozen squares of glass into one; one shopman into a dozen; and there is no knowing what would have been done, if it had not been fortunately discovered, just in time, that the Commissioners of Bankruptcy were as competent to decide such cases as the Commissioners of Lunacy, and that a little confinement and gentle examination did wonders. The disease abated. It died away. A year or two of comparative tranquillity ensued. Suddenly it burst out again among the chemists; the symptoms were the same, with the addition of a strong desire to stick the royal arms over the shop-door, and a great rage for mahogany, varnish, and expensive floor-cloth. Then, the hosiers were infected, and began to pull down their shop-fronts with frantic recklessness. The mania again died away, and the public began to congratulate themselves on its entire disappearance, when it burst forth with tenfold violence among the publicans, and keepers of "wine vaults." From that moment it has spread among them with unprecedented rapidity, exhibiting a con-catenation of all the previous symptoms; onward it has rushed to every part of town, knocking down all the old public-houses, and depositing splendid mansions, stone balustrades, rosewood fittings, immense lamps, and illuminated clocks, at the corner of every street.

The extensive scale on which these places are established, and the ostentatious manner in which the business of even the smallest among them is divided into branches, is amusing. A handsome plate of ground glass in one door directs you "To the Counting-house"; another to the "Bottle Department"; a third to the "Wholesale Department"; a fourth to "The Wine Promenade"; and so forth, until we are in daily expectation of meeting with a "Brandy Bell," or a "Whiskey Entrance." Then, ingenuity is exhausted in devising attractive titles for the different descriptions of gin; and the dram-drinking portion of the community as they gaze upon the gigantic black and white announcements, which are only to be equalled in size by the figures beneath them, are left in a state of pleasing hesitation between "The Cream of the Valley," "The Out and Out," "The No Mistake," "The Good for Mixing," "The real Knock-me-down," "The celebrated Butter Gin," "The regular Flare-up," and a dozen other, equally inviting and wholesome *liqueurs*. Although places of this description are to be met with in every second street, they are invariably numerous and splendid in precise proportion to the dirt and poverty of the surrounding neighbourhood. The gin-shops in and near Drury Lane, Holborn, St. Giles's, Covent Garden, and Clare Market, are the handsomest in London. There is more of filth and squalid misery near those great thoroughfares than in any part of this mighty city.

We will endeavour to sketch the bar of a large gin-shop, and its ordinary customers, for the edification of such of our readers as may not have had opportunities of observing such scenes; and on the chance of finding one well suited to our purpose, we will make for Drury Lane, through the narrow streets and dirty courts which divide it from Oxford Street, and that classical spot adjoining the brewery at the bottom of Tottenham

Court Road, best known to the initiated as the "Rookery."

The filthy and miserable appearance of this part of London can hardly be imagined by those (and there are many such) who have not witnessed it. Wretched houses with broken windows patched with rags and paper: every room let out to a different family, and in many instances to two or even three—fruit and "sweet-stuff" manufacturers in the cellars, barbers and red-herring vendors in the front-parlours, cobblers in the back; a bird-fancier in the first-floor, three families on the second, starvation in the attics, Irishmen in the passage, a "musician" in the front-kitchen, and a char-woman and five hungry children in the back one—filth everywhere—a gutter before the houses and a drain behind—clothes drying and slops emptying, from the windows; girls of fourteen or fifteen, with matted hair, walking about barefoot, and in white greatcoats, almost their only covering; boys of all ages, in coats of all sizes and no coats at all; men and women, in every variety of scanty and dirty apparel, lounging, scolding, drinking, smoking, squabbling, fighting, and swearing.

You turn the corner. What a change! All is light and brilliancy. The hum of many voices issues from that splendid gin-shop which forms the commencement of the two streets opposite; and the gay building with the fantastically ornamented parapet, the illuminated clock, the plate-glass windows surrounded by stucco rosettes, and its profusion of gas-lights in richly-gilt burners, is perfectly dazzling when contrasted with the darkness and dirt we have just left. The interior is even gayer than the exterior. A bar of French-polished mahogany, elegantly carved, extends the whole width of

THE GIN-SHOP

the place; and there are two side-aisles of great casks, painted green and gold, enclosed within a light brass rail, and bearing such inscriptions as "Old Tom, 549"; "Young Tom, 360"; "Samson, 1421"—the figures agreeing, we presume, with "gallons," understand. Beyond the bar is a lofty and spacious saloon, full of the same enticing vessels, with a gallery running round it, equally well furnished. On the counter, in addition to the usual spirit apparatus, are two or three little baskets of cakes and biscuits, which are carefully secured at top with wickerwork, to prevent their contents being unlawfully abstracted. Behind it are two showily-dressed damsels with large necklaces, dispensing the spirits and "compounds." They are assisted by the ostensible proprietor of the concern, a stout coarse fellow in a fur cap, put on very much on one side to give him a knowing air, and to display his sandy whiskers to the best advantage.

The two old washerwomen, who are seated on the little bench to the left of the bar, are rather overcome by the headdresses and haughty demeanour of the young ladies who officiate. They receive their half-quartern of gin and peppermint with considerable deference, prefacing a request for "one of them soft biscuits," with a "Jist be good enough, ma'am." They are quite astonished at the impudent air of the young fellow in a brown coat and bright buttons, who, ushering in his two companions, and walking up to the bar in as careless a manner as if he had been used to green and gold ornaments all his life, winks at one of the young ladies with singular coolness, and calls for a "kervorten and a three-out-glass," just as if the place were his own. "Gin for you, sir?" says the young lady when she has drawn it: carefully looking every way but the right one, to show that the wink had no effect upon her. "For me, Mary, my dear," replies the gentleman in brown. "My name an't Mary as it happens," says the young girl, rather relaxing as she delivers the change. "Well, if it an't, it ought to be," responds the irresistible one; "all the Marys as ever *I* see, was handsome gals." Here the young lady, not precisely remembering how blushes are managed in such cases, abruptly ends the flirtation by addressing the female in the faded feathers who has just entered, and who, after stating explicitly, to prevent any subsequent misunderstanding, that "this gentleman pays," calls for "a glass of port wine and a bit of sugar."

Those two old men who came in "just to have a drain," finished their third quartern a few seconds ago; they have made themselves crying drunk; and the fat comfortable-looking elderly women, who had "a glass of rum-srub" each, having chimed in with their complaints on the hardness of the times, one of the women has agreed to stand a glass round, jocularly observing that "grief never mended no broken bones, and as good people's wery scarce, what I says is, make the most on 'em, and that's all about it!" a sentiment which appears to afford unlimited satisfaction to those who have nothing to pay.

It is growing late, and the throng of men, women, and children, who have been constantly going in and out, dwindles down to two or three occasional stragglers— cold, wretched-looking creatures, in the last stage of emaciation and disease. The knot of Irish labourers at the lower end of the place, who have been alternately shaking hands with, and threatening the life of each other, for the last hour, become furious in their disputes, and finding it impossible to silence one man, who is particularly anxious to adjust the difference, they resort to the expedient of knocking him down and jumping on him afterwards. The man in the fur cap and the potboy rush out; a scene of riot and confusion ensues; half the Irishmen get shut out, and the other half get shut in; the potboy is knocked among the tubs in no time; the landlord hits everybody, and everybody hits the landlord; the barmaids scream; the police come in; the rest is a confused mixture of arms, legs, staves, torn coats, shouting, and struggling. Some of the party are borne off to the station-house, and the remainder slink home to beat their wives for complaining, and kick the children for daring to be hungry.

We have sketched this subject very slightly, not only because our limits compel us to do so, but because, if it were pursued farther, it would be painful and repulsive. Well-disposed gentlemen, and charitable ladies, would alike turn with coldness and disgust from a description of the drunken besotted men, and wretched broken-down miserable women, who form no inconsiderable portion of the frequenters of these haunts; forgetting, in the pleasant consciousness of their own rectitude, the poverty of the one, and the temptation of the other. Gin-drinking is a great vice in England, but wretchedness and dirt are a greater; and until you improve the homes of the poor, or persuade a half-famished wretch not to seek relief in the temporary oblivion of his own misery, with the pittance which, divided among his family, would furnish a morsel of bread for each, gin-shops will increase in number and splendour. If Temperance Societies would suggest an antidote against hunger, filth, and foul air, or could establish dispensaries for the gratuitous distribution of bottles of Lethe-water, gin-palaces would be numbered among the things that were.

GREENWICH FAIR

If the parks be "the lungs of London," we wonder what Greenwich Fair is—a periodical breaking out, we suppose, a sort of spring-rash: a three days' fever, which cools the blood for six months afterwards, and at the expiration of which London is restored to its old habits of plodding industry, as suddenly and completely as if nothing had ever happened to disturb them.

In our earlier days, we were a constant frequenter of Greenwich Fair, for years. We have proceeded to, and returned from it, in almost every description of vehicle. We cannot conscientiously deny the charge of having once made the passage in a spring-van, accompanied by thirteen gentlemen, fourteen ladies, an unlimited number of children, and a barrel of beer; and we have a vague recollection of having, in later days, found ourself the eighth outside, on the top of a hackney-coach, at something past four o'clock in the morning, with a rather confused idea of our own name, or place of residence. We have grown older since then, and quiet, and steady: liking nothing better than to spend our Easter, and all our other holidays, in some quiet nook, with people of whom we shall never tire; but we think we still remember something of Greenwich Fair, and of those who resort to it. At all events we will try.

The road to Greenwich during the whole of Easter Monday is in a state of perpetual bustle and noise. Cabs, hackney-coaches, "shay" carts, coal-waggons, stages, omnibuses, sociables, gigs, donkey-chaises—all crammed with people (for the question never is, what the horse can draw, but what the vehicle will hold)—roll along at their utmost speed; the dust flies in clouds, ginger-beer corks go off in volleys, the balcony of every public-house is crowded with people, smoking and drinking, half the private houses are turned into tea-shops, fiddles are in great request, every little fruit-shop displays its stall of gilt gingerbread and penny toys; turnpike men are in despair; horses won't go on, and wheels will come off; ladies in "carawans" scream with fright at every fresh concussion, and their admirers find it necessary to sit remarkably close to them, by way of encouragement; servants of all work, who are not allowed to have followers, and have got a holiday for the day, make the most of their time with the faithful admirer who waits for a stolen interview at the corner of the street every night, when they go to fetch the beer—apprentices grow sentimental, and straw-bonnet makers kind. Everybody is anxious to get on, and actuated by the common wish to be at the fair, or in the park, as soon as possible.

Pedestrians linger in groups at the roadside, unable to resist the allurements of the stout proprietress of the "Jack-in-the-box, three shies a penny," or the more splendid offers of the man with three thimbles and a pea on a little round board, who astonishes the be-wildered crowd with some such address as, "Here's the sort o' game to make you laugh seven years arter you're dead, and turn ev'ry air on your ed gray vith delight! Three thimbles and vun little pea—with a vun, two, three, and a two, three, vun: catch him who can, look on, keep your eyes open, and niver say die! niver mind the change, and the expense: all fair and above board: them as don't play can't vin, and luck attend the ryal sportsman! Bet any gen'lm'n any sum of money, from harf-a-crown up to a suverin, as he doesn't name the thimble as kivers the pea!" Here some greenhorn whispers his friend that he distinctly saw the pea roll under the middle thimble—an impression which is immediately confirmed by a gentleman in top-boots, who is standing by, and who, in a low tone, regrets his own inability to bet, in consequence of having unfortunately left his purse at home, but strongly urges the stranger not to neglect such a golden opportunity. The "plant" is successful, the bet is made, the stranger of course loses: and the gentleman with the thimbles consoles him, as he pockets the money, with an assurance that it's "all the fortin of war! this time I vin, next time you vin: niver mind the loss of two bob and a bender! Do it up in a small parcel, and break out in a fresh place. Here's the sort o' game," &c.—and the eloquent harangue, with such variations as the speaker's exuberant fancy suggests, is again repeated to the gaping crowd, reinforced by the accession of several new-comers.

The chief place of resort in the daytime, after the public-houses, is the park, in which the principal amusement is to drag young ladies up the steep hill which leads to the Observatory, and then drag them down again, at the very top of their speed, greatly to the derangement of their curls and bonnet-caps, and much to the edification of lookers-on from below. "Kiss in the Ring," and "Threading my Grandmother's Needle," too, are sports which receive their full share of pat-ronage. Love-sick swains, under the influence of gin-and-water, and the tender passion, become violently affectionate: and the fair objects of their regard enhance the value of stolen kisses by a vast deal of struggling, and holding down of heads, and cries of "Oh! Ha' done, then, George—Oh, do tickle him for me, Mary—Well, I never!" and similar Lucretian ejaculations. Little old men and women, with a small basket under one arm, and a wine-glass, without a foot, in the other hand, tender "a drop o' the right sort" to the different groups; and young ladies, who are persuaded to indulge in a drop of the aforesaid right sort, display a pleasing degree of reluctance to taste it, and cough afterwards with great propriety.

The old pensioners, who, for the moderate charge of a penny, exhibit the mast-house, the Thames and shipping, the place where the men used to hang in chains, and other interesting sights, through a telescope, are asked questions about objects within the range of the glass, which it would puzzle a Solomon to answer; and requested to find out particular houses in particular streets, which it would have been a task of some difficulty for Mr. Horner (not the young gentleman who ate mince-pies with his thumb, but the man of Colosseum notoriety) to discover. Here and there, where some three or four couples are sitting on the grass together, you will see a sunburnt woman in a red cloak "telling fortunes" and prophesying husbands, which it requires no extraordinary observation to describe, for the originals are before her. Thereupon, the lady concerned laughs and blushes, and ultimately buries her face in an imitation cambric handkerchief, and the gentleman described looks extremely foolish, and squeezes her hand, and fees the gipsy liberally; and the gipsy goes away, perfectly satisfied herself, and leaving those behind her perfectly satisfied also: and the prophecy, like many other prophecies of greater importance, fulfils itself in time.

But it grows dark: the crowd has gradually dispersed,

and only a few stragglers are left behind. The light in the direction of the church shows that the fair is illuminated; and the distant noise proves it to be filling fast. The spot, which half an hour ago was ringing with the shouts of boisterous mirth, is as calm and quiet as if nothing could ever disturb its serenity; the fine old trees, the majestic building at their feet, with the noble river beyond, glistening in the moonlight, appear in all their beauty, and under their most favourable aspect; the voices of the boys, singing their evening hymn, are borne gently on the air; and the humblest mechanic who has been lingering on the grass so pleasant to the feet that beat the same dull round from week to week in the paved streets of London, feels proud to think as he surveys the scene before him, that he belongs to the country which has selected such a spot as a retreat for its oldest and best defenders in the decline of their lives.

Five minutes' walking brings you to the fair; a scene calculated to awaken very different feelings. The entrance is occupied on either side by the vendors of gingerbread and toys: the stalls are gaily lighted up, the most attractive goods profusely disposed, and unbonneted young ladies, in their zeal for the interest of their employers, seize you by the coat, and use all the blandishments of "Do, dear"—"There's a love"—"Don't be cross, now," &c., to induce you to purchase half a pound of the real spice nuts, of which the majority of the regular fair-goers carry a pound or two as a present supply, tied up in a cotton pocket-handkerchief. Occasionally you pass a deal table, on which are exposed penn'orths of pickled salmon (fennel included), in little white saucers: oysters, with shells as large as cheese-plates, and divers specimens of a species of snail (*wilks*, we think they are called), floating in a somewhat bilious-looking green liquid. Cigars, too, are in great demand; gentlemen must smoke, of course, and here they are, two a penny, in a regular authentic cigar-box, with a lighted tallow candle in the centre.

Imagine yourself in an extremely dense crowd, which swings you to and fro, and in and out, and every way but the right one; add to this the screams of women, the shouts of boys, the clanging of gongs, the firing of pistols, the ringing of bells, the bellowings of speaking-trumpets, the squeaking of penny dittoes, the noise of a dozen bands, with three drums in each, all playing different tunes at the same time, the hallooing of showmen, and an occasional roar from the wild-beast shows; and you are in the very centre and heart of the fair.

This immense booth, with the large stage in front, so brightly illuminated with variegated lamps, and pots of burning fat, is "Richardson's," where you have a melo-drama (with three murders and a ghost), a pantomime, a comic song, an overture, and some incidental music, all done in five-and-twenty minutes.

The company are now promenading outside in all the dignity of wigs, spangles, red-ochre, and whitening. See with what a ferocious air the gentleman who personates the Mexican chief paces up and down, and with what an eye of calm dignity the principal tragedian gazes on the crowd below, or converses confidentially with the harlequin! The four clowns, who are engaged in a mock broadsword combat, may be all very well for the low-minded holiday-makers; but these are the people for the reflective portion of the community. They look so noble in those Roman dresses, with their yellow legs and arms, long black curly heads, bushy eyebrows, and scowl expressive of assassination, and vengeance, and everything else that is grand and solemn. Then, the ladies—were there ever such innocent and awful-looking beings; as they walk up and down the platform in twos and threes, with their arms round each other's waists, or leaning for support on one of those majestic men! Their spangled muslin dresses and blue satin shoes and sandals (a *leetle* the worse for wear) are the admiration of all beholders; and the playful manner in which they check the advances of the clown is perfectly enchanting.

"Just a-going to begin! Pray come for'erd, come for'erd," exclaims the man in the countryman's dress, for the seventieth time: and people force their way up the steps in crowds. The band suddenly strikes up, the harlequin and columbine set the example, reels are formed in less than no time, the Roman heroes place their arms akimbo, and dance with considerable agility; and the leading tragic actress, and the gentleman who enacts the "swell" in the pantomime, foot it to perfection. "All in to begin," shouts the manager, when no more people can be induced to "come for'erd," and away rush the leading members of the company to do the dreadful in the first piece.

A change of performance takes place every day during the fair, but the story of the tragedy is always pretty much the same. There is a rightful heir, who loves a young lady, and is beloved by her; and a wrongful heir, who loves her too, and isn't beloved by her; and the wrongful heir gets hold of the rightful heir, and throws him into a dungeon, just to kill him off when convenient, for which purpose he hires a couple of assassins—a good one and a bad one—who, the moment they are left alone, get up a little murder on their own account, the good one killing the bad one, and the bad one wounding the good one. Then the rightful heir is discovered in prison, carefully holding a long chain in his hands, and seated despondingly in a large arm-chair; and the young lady comes in to two bars of soft music, and embraces the rightful heir; and then the wrongful heir comes in to two bars of quick music (technically called "a hurry"), and goes on in the most shocking manner, throwing the young lady about as if she was nobody, and calling the rightful heir "Ar-recreant—ar-wretch!" in a very loud voice, which answers the double purpose of displaying his passion, and preventing the sound being deadened by the sawdust. The interest becomes intense; the wrongful heir draws his sword, and rushes on the rightful heir; a blue smoke is seen, a gong is heard, and a tall white figure (who has been all this time behind the arm-chair, covered over with a table-cloth) slowly rises to the tune of "Oft in the stilly night." This is no other than the ghost of the rightful heir's father, who was killed by the wrongful heir's father, at sight of which the wrongful heir becomes apoplectic, and is literally "struck all of a heap," the stage not being large enough to admit of his falling down at full length. Then the good assassin staggers in, and says he was hired in conjunction with the bad assassin, by the wrongful heir, to kill the rightful heir; and he's killed a good many people in his time, but he's very sorry for it, and won't do so any more—a promise which he immediately redeems, by dying off-hand without any nonsense about it. Then the rightful heir throws down his chain; and then two men, a sailor, and a young woman (the tenantry of the rightful heir) come in, and the ghost makes dumb motions to them, which they, by supernatural interference, understand—for no one else can; and the ghost (who can't do anything without blue fire) blesses the rightful heir and the young lady, by half suffocating them with smoke: and then a muffin-bell rings, and the curtain drops.

The exhibitions next in popularity to these itinerant theatres are the travelling menageries, or, to speak more intelligibly, the "Wild-beast shows," where a military band in beefeaters' costume, with leopard-skin caps, play incessantly; and where large highly-coloured representations of tigers tearing men's heads open, and a lion being burnt with red-hot irons to induce him to drop his victim, are hung up outside, by way of attracting visitors.

The principal officer at these places is generally a very tall, hoarse man, in a scarlet coat, with a cane in his hand, with which he occasionally raps the pictures we have just noticed, by way of illustrating his description—something in this way. "Here, here, here; the lion, the lion (tap), exactly as he is represented on the canvas outside (three taps): no waiting, remember; no deception. The fe-ro-cious lion (tap, tap) who bit off the gentleman's head last Cambervel vos a twelve-month, and has killed on the awerage three keepers a year ever since he arrived at matoority. No extra charge on this account recollect; the price of admission is only sixpence." This address never fails to produce a considerable sensation, and sixpences flow into the treasury with wonderful rapidity.

The dwarfs are also objects of great curiosity, and as a dwarf, a giantess, a living skeleton, a wild Indian, "a young lady of singular beauty, with perfectly white hair and pink eyes," and two or three other natural curiosities, are usually exhibited together for the small charge of a penny, they attract very numerous audiences. The best thing about a dwarf is that he has always a little box, about two feet six inches high, into which, by long practice, he can just manage to get, by doubling himself up like a boot-jack; this box is painted outside like a six-roomed house, and as the crowd see him ring a bell, or fire a pistol out of the first-floor window, they verily believe that it is his ordinary town residence, divided like other mansions into drawing-rooms, dining-parlour, and bed-chambers. Shut up in this case, the unfortunate little object is brought out to delight the throng by holding a facetious dialogue with the proprietor: in the course of which, the dwarf (who is always particularly drunk) pledges himself to sing a comic song inside, and pays various compliments to the ladies, which induce them to "come for'erd" with great alacrity. As a giant is not so easily moved, a pair of in-describables of most capacious dimensions, and a huge shoe, are usually brought out, into which two or three stout men get all at once, to the enthusiastic delight of the crowd, who are quite satisfied with the solemn assurance that these habiliments form part of the giant's everyday costume.

The grandest and most numerously-frequented booth in the whole fair, however, is "the Grown and Anchor"—a temporary ball-room—we forget how many hundred feet long, the price of admission to which is one shilling. Immediately on your right hand as you enter, after paying your money, is a refreshment place, at which cold beef, roast and boiled, French rolls, stout, wine, tongue, ham, even fowls, if we recollect right, are displayed in tempting array. There is a raised orchestra, and the place is boarded all the way down, in patches, just wide enough for a country dance.

GREENWICH FAIR

There is no master of the ceremonies in this artificial Eden—all is primitive, unreserved, and unstudied. The dust is blinding, the heat insupportable, the company somewhat noisy, and in the highest spirits possible: the ladies, in the height of their innocent animation, dancing in the gentlemen's hats, and the gentlemen promenading the "gay and festive scene" in the ladies' bonnets, or with the more expensive ornaments of false noses, and low-crowned, tinder-box-looking hats: playing children's drums, and accompanied by ladies on the penny trumpet.

The noise of these various instruments, the orchestra, the shouting, the "scratchers," and the dancing, is perfectly bewildering. The dancing, itself, beggars description—every figure lasts about an hour, and the ladies bounce up and down the middle, with a degree of spirit which is quite indescribable. As to the gentlemen, they stamp their feet against the ground, every time "hands four round" begins, go down the middle and up again, with cigars in their mouths, and silk handkerchiefs in their hands, and whirl their partners round, nothing loth, scrambling and falling, and embracing, and knocking up against the other couples, until they are fairly tired out, and can move no longer. The same scene is repeated again and again (slightly varied by an occasional "row") until a late hour at night: and a great many clerks and 'prentices find themselves next morning with aching heads, empty pockets, damaged hats, and a very imperfect recollection of how it was they did *not* get home.

THE PAWNBROKER'S SHOP

Of the numerous receptacles for misery and distress with which the streets of London unhappily abound, there are, perhaps, none which present such striking scenes as the pawnbrokers' shops. The very nature and description of these places occasion their being but little known, except to the unfortunate beings whose profligacy or misfortune drives them to seek the temporary relief they offer. The subject may appear, at first sight, to be anything but an inviting one, but we venture on it nevertheless, in the hope that, as far as the limits of our present papers are concerned, it will present nothing to disgust even the most fastidious reader.

There are some pawnbrokers' shops of a very superior description. There are grades in pawning as in everything else, and distinctions must be observed even in poverty. The aristocratic Spanish cloak and the plebeian calico shirt, the silver fork and the flat-iron, the muslin cravat and the Belcher, neckerchief, would but ill assort together; so, the better sort of pawnbroker calls himself a silversmith, and decorates his shop with handsome trinkets and expensive jewellery, while the more humble money-lender boldly advertises his calling, and invites observation. It is with pawnbrokers' shops of the latter class that we have to do. We have selected one for our purpose, and will endeavour to describe it.

The pawnbroker's shop is situated near Drury Lane,

at the corner of a court, which affords a side entrance for the accommodation of such customers as may be desirous of avoiding the observation of the passers-by, or the chance of recognition in the public street. It is a low, dirty-looking, dusty shop, the door of which stands always doubtfully, a little way open: half inviting, half repelling the hesitating visitor, who, if he be as yet uninitiated, examines one of the old garnet brooches in the window for a minute or two with affected eagerness, as if he contemplated making a purchase; and then looking cautiously round to ascertain that no one watches him, hastily slinks in: the door closing of itself after him, to just its former width. The shop-front and the window-frames bear evident marks of having been once painted; but, what the colour was originally or at what date it was probably laid on, are at this remote period questions which may be asked, but cannot be answered. Tradition states that the transparency in the front door, which displays at night three red balls on a blue ground, once bore also, inscribed in graceful waves, the words "Money advanced on plate, jewels, wearing apparel, and every description of property," but a few illegible hieroglyphics are all that now remain to attest the fact. The plate and jewels would seem to have disappeared, together with the announcement, for the articles of stock, which are displayed in some profusion in the window, do not include any very valuable luxuries of either kind. A few old china cups; some modern vases, adorned with paltry paintings of three Spanish cavaliers playing three Spanish guitars; or a party of boors car-ousing: each boor with one leg painfully elevated in the air, by way of expressing his perfect freedom and gaiety; several sets of chessmen, two or three flutes, a few fiddles, a round-eyed portrait staring in astonishment from a very dark ground; some gaudily-bound prayer-books and testaments, two rows of silver watches quite as clumsy and almost as large as Ferguson's first; numerous old-fashioned table and tea spoons, displayed, fan-like, in half-dozens; strings of coral with great broad gilt snaps; cards of rings and brooches, fastened and labelled separately, like the insects in the British Museum; cheap silver penholders and snuffboxes, with a masonic star, complete the jewellery department; while five or six beds in smeary clouded ticks, strings of blankets and sheets, silk and cotton handkerchiefs, and wearing apparel of every description, form the more useful, though even less ornamental, part of the articles exposed for sale. An extensive collection of planes, chisels, saws, and other carpenters' tools, which have been pledged, and never redeemed, form the foreground of the picture; while the large frames full of ticketed bundles, which are dimly seen through the dirty casement upstairs—the squalid neighbourhood—the adjoining houses, straggling, shrunken, and rotten, with one or two filthy, unwhole-some-looking heads thrust out of every window, and old red pans and stunted plants exposed on the tottering parapets, to the manifest hazard of the heads of the passers-by—the noisy men loitering under the archway at the corner of the court, or about the gin-shop next door—and their wives patiently standing on the curb-stone, with large baskets of cheap vegetables slung round them for sale, are its immediate auxiliaries.

If the outside of the pawnbroker's shop be calculated to attract the attention, or excite the interest, of the speculative pedestrian, its interior cannot fail to produce the same effect in an increased degree. The front door, which we have before noticed, opens into the common shop, which is the resort of all those customers whose habitual acquaintance with such scenes renders them indifferent to the observation of their companions in poverty. The side door opens into a small passage from which some half-dozen doors (which may be secured on the inside by bolts) open into a corresponding number of little dens, or closets, which face the counter. Here, the more timid or respectable portion of the crowd shroud themselves from the notice of the remainder, and patiently wait until the gentleman behind the counter, with the curly black hair, diamond ring, and double silver watch-guard, shall feel disposed to favour them with his notice—a consummation which depends considerably on the temper of the aforesaid gentleman for the time being.

At the present moment, this elegantly-attired individual is in the act of entering the duplicate he had just made out, in a thick book: a process from which he is diverted occasionally by a conversation he is carrying on with another young man similarly employed at a little distance from him, whose allusions to "that last bottle of soda-water last night," and "how regularly round my hat he felt himself when the young 'ooman gave 'em in charge," would appear to refer to the consequences of some stolen joviality of the preceding evening. The customers generally, however, seem unable to participate in the amusement derivable from this source, for an old sallow-looking woman, who has been leaning with both arms on the counter with a small bundle before her, for half-an-hour previously, suddenly interrupts the conversation by addressing the jewelled shopman—"Now, Mr. Henry, do make haste, there's a good soul, for my two grandchildren's locked up at home, and I'm afeer'd of the fire." The shopman

THE PAWNBROKER'S SHOP

slightly raises his head, with an air of deep abstraction, and resumes his entry with as much deliberation as if he were engraving. "You're in a hurry, Mrs. Tatham, this ev'nin', an't you?" is the only notice he deigns to take, after the lapse of five minutes or so. "Yes, I am indeed, Mr. Henry; now, do serve me next, there's a good creetur. I wouldn't worry you, only it's all along o' them botherin' children." "What have you got here?" inquires the shopman, unpinning the bundle—"old concern, I suppose—pair o' stays and a petticut. You must look up somethin' else, old 'ooman; I can't lend you anything more upon them; they're completely worn out by this time, if it's only by putting in, and taking out again, three times a week." "Oh! you're a rum 'un, you are," replies the old woman, laughing extremely, as in duty bound; "I wish I'd got the gift of the gab like you; see if I'd be up the spout so often then! No, no; it an't the petticut; it's a child's frock and a beautiful silk-ankecher, as belongs to my husband. He gave four shillin' for it, the werry same blessed day as he broke his arm."—"What do you want upon these?" inquires Mr. Henry, slightly glancing at the articles, which in all probability are old acquaintances. "What do you want upon these?"—"Eighteen-pence."—"Lend you ninepence."—"Oh, make it a shillin'; there's a dear—do now!"—"Not another farden."—"Well, I suppose I must take it." The duplicate is made out, one ticket pinned on the parcel, the other given to the old woman; the parcel is flung carelessly down into a corner, and some other customer prefers his claim to be served without further delay.

The choice falls on an unshaven, dirty, sottish-looking fellow, whose tarnished paper-cap, stuck negligently over one eye, communicates an additionally repulsive expression to his very uninviting countenance. He was enjoying a little relaxation from his sedentary pursuits a quarter of an hour ago, in kicking his wife up the court. He has come to redeem some tools:— probably to complete a job with, on account of which he has already received some money, if his inflamed countenance and drunken stagger may be taken as evidence of the fact. Having waited some little time, he makes his presence known by venting his ill-humour on a ragged urchin, who, being unable to bring his face on a level with the counter by any other process, has employed himself in climbing up, and then hooking himself on with his elbows—an uneasy perch, from which he has fallen at intervals, generally alighting on the toes of the person in his immediate vicinity. In the present case, the unfortunate little wretch has received a cuff which sends him reeling to the door; and the donor of the blow is immediately the object of general indignation.

"What do you strike the boy for, you brute?" exclaims a slipshod woman, with two flat-irons in a little basket. "Do you think he's your wife, you willin?" "Go and hang yourself!" replies the gentleman addressed, with a drunken look of savage stupidity, aiming at the same time a blow at the woman which fortunately misses its object. "Go and hang yourself; and wait till I come and cut you down."—"Cut you down," rejoins the woman, "I wish I had the cutting of you up, you wagabond! (loud.) Oh! you precious wagabond! (rather louder.) Where's your wife, you willin? (louder still; women of this class are always sympathetic, and work themselves into a tremendous passion on the shortest notice.) Your poor dear wife as you uses worser nor a dog—strike a woman—you a man! (very shrill) I wish I had you—I'd murder you, I would, if I died for it!"— "Now be civil," retorts the man fiercely. "Be civil, you wiper!" ejaculates the woman contemptuously. "An't it shocking?" she continues, turning round, and appealing to an old woman who is peeping out of one of the little closets we have before described, and who has not the slightest objection to join in the attack, possessing, as she does, the comfortable conviction that she is bolted in. "An't it shocking, ma'am? (Dreadful! says the old woman in a parenthesis, not exactly knowing what the question refers to.) He's got a wife, ma'am, as takes in mangling, and is as 'dustrious and hard-working a young 'ooman as can be, (very fast) as lives in the back-parlour of our 'ous, which my husband and me lives in the front one (with great rapidity)—and we hears him a-beaten' on her sometimes when he comes home drunk, the whole night through, and not only a-beaten' her, but beaten' his own child too, to make her more miserable—ugh, you beast! and she, poor creater, won't swear the peace agin him, nor do nothin', because she likes the wretch arter all—worse luck!" Here, as the woman has completely run herself out of breath, the pawn-broker himself, who has just appeared behind the counter, in a grey dressing-gown, embraces the favourable opportunity of putting in a word:—"Now I won't have none of this sort of thing on my premises!" he interposes with an air of authority. "Mrs. Mackin, keep yourself to yourself, or you don't get fourpence for a flat-iron here; and Jinkins, you leave your ticket here till you're sober, and send your wife for them two planes, for I won't have you in my shop at no price; so make yourself scarce, before I make you scarcer."

This eloquent address produces anything but the effect desired; the women rail in concert; the man hits about him in all directions, and is in the act of establishing an indisputable claim to gratuitous lodgings for the night, when the entrance of his wife, a wretched worn-out woman, apparently in the last stage of consumption, whose face bears evident marks of recent ill-usage, and whose strength seems hardly equal to the burden—light enough, God knows!—of the thin, sickly child she carries in her arms, turns his cowardly rage in a safer direction. "Come home, dear," cries the miserable creature, in an imploring tone; "*do* come home, there's a good fellow, and go to bed."—"Go home yourself," rejoins the furious ruffian. "Do come home quietly," repeats the wife, bursting into tears. "Go home yourself," retorts the husband again, enforcing his argument by a blow which sends the poor creature flying out of the shop. Her "natural protector" follows her up the court, alternately venting his rage in accelerating her progress, and in knocking the little scanty blue bonnet of the unfortunate child over its still more scanty and faded-looking face.

In the last box, which is situated in the darkest and most obscure corner of the shop, considerably removed from either of the gas-lights, are a young delicate girl of about twenty and an elderly female, evidently her mother from the resemblance between them, who stand at some distance back, as if to avoid the observation even of the shopman. It is not their first visit to a pawnbroker's shop, for they answer without a moment's hesitation the usual questions, put in a rather respectful manner, and in a much lower tone than usual, of "What name shall I say?—Your own property, of course?—Where do you live?—Housekeeper or lodger?" They bargain, too, for a higher loan than the shopman is at first inclined to offer, which a perfect stranger would be little disposed to do; and the elder female urges her daughter on, in scarcely audible whispers, to exert her utmost powers of persuasion to obtain an advance of the sum, and expatiate on the value of the articles they have brought to raise a present supply upon. They are a small gold chain and a "Forget-me-not" ring: the girl's property, for they are both too small for the mother; given her in better times; prized, perhaps, once, for the giver's sake, but parted with now without a struggle; for want has hardened the mother, and her example has hardened the girl, and the prospect of receiving money, coupled with a recollection of the misery they have both endured from the want of it—the coldness of old friends—the stern refusal of some, and the still more galling compassion of others—appears to have obliterated the consciousness of self-humiliation, which the idea of their present situation would once have aroused.

In the next box is a young female, whose attire, miserably poor, but extremely gaudy, wretchedly cold but extravagantly fine, too plainly bespeaks her station. The rich satin gown with its faded trimmings, the worn-out thin shoes, and pink silk stockings, the summer bonnet in winter, and the sunken face, where a daub of rouge only serves as an index to the ravages of squandered health never to be regained, and lost happiness never to be restored, and where the practised smile is a wretched mockery of the misery of the heart, cannot be mistaken. There is something in the glimpse she has just caught of her young neighbour, and in the sight of the little trinkets she has offered in pawn, that seems to have awakened in this woman's mind some slumbering recollection, and to have changed, for an instant, her whole demeanour. Her first hasty impulse was to bend forward as if to scan more minutely the appearance of her half-concealed companions; her next, on seeing them involuntarily shrink from her, to retreat to the back of the box, cover her face with her hands, and burst into tears.

There are strange chords in the human heart, which will lie dormant through years of depravity and wickedness, but which will vibrate at last to some slight circumstance apparently trivial in itself, but connected by some undefined and indistinct association, with past days that can never be recalled, and with bitter recollections from which the most degraded creature in existence cannot escape.

There has been another spectator, in the person of a woman in the common shop; the lowest of the low; dirty, unbonneted, flaunting, and slovenly. Her curiosity was at first attracted by the little she could see of the group; then her attention. The half-intoxicated leer changed to an expression of something like interest, and a feeling similar to that we have described appeared for a moment, and only a moment, to extend itself even to her bosom.

Who shall say how soon these women may change places? The last has but two more stages—the hospital and the grave. How many females situated as her two companions are, and as she may have been once, have terminated the same wretched course, in the same wretched manner? One is already tracing her footsteps with frightful rapidity. How soon may the other follow her example? How many have done the same?

The Last Cab-Driver,
and the First Omnibus Cad

Of all the cabriolet-drivers whom we have ever had the honour and gratification of knowing by sight—and our acquaintance in this way has been most extensive—there is one who made an impression on our mind which can never be effaced, and who awakened in our bosom a feeling of admiration and respect, which we entertain a fatal presentiment will never be called forth again by any human being. He was a man of most simple and prepossessing appearance. He was a brown-whiskered, white-hatted, no-coated cabman; his nose was generally red, and his bright blue eye not unfrequently stood out in bold relief against a black border of artificial workmanship; his boots were of the Wellington form, pulled up to meet his corduroy knee-smalls, or at least to approach as near them as their dimensions would admit of; and his neck was usually garnished with a bright yellow handkerchief. In summer he carried in his mouth a flower; in winter, a straw—slight, but to a contemplative mind, certain indications of a love of nature, and a taste for botany.

His cabriolet was gorgeously painted—a bright red; and wherever we went, City or West End, Paddington or Holloway, North, East, West, or South, there was the red cab, bumping up against the posts at the street-corners, and turning in and out, among hackney-coaches, and drays, and carts, and waggons, and omnibuses, and contriving by some strange means or other to get out of places which no other vehicle but the red cab could ever by any possibility have contrived to get into at all. Our fondness for that red cab was unbounded. How we should have liked to have seen it in the circle at Astley's! Our life upon it, that it should have performed such evolutions as would have put the whole company to shame—Indian chiefs, knights, Swiss peasants, and all.

Some people object to the exertion of getting into cabs, and others object to the difficulty of getting out of them; we think both these are objections which take their rise in perverse and ill-conditioned minds. The getting into a cab is a very pretty and graceful process, which, when well performed, is essentially melodramatic. First, there is the expressive pantomime of every one of the eighteen cabmen on the stand, the moment you raise your eyes from the ground. Then there is your own pantomime in reply—quite a little ballet. Four cabs immediately leave the stand, for your especial accommodation; and the evolutions of the animals who draw them are beautiful in the extreme, as they grate the wheels of the cabs against the curb-stones, and sport playfully in the kennel. You single out a particular cab, and dart swiftly towards it. One bound, and you are on the first step; turn your body lightly round to the right, and you are on the second; bend gracefully beneath the reins, working round to the left at the same time, and you are in the cab. There is no difficulty in finding a seat: the apron knocks you comfortably into it at once, and off you go.

The getting out of a cab is, perhaps, rather more complicated in its theory, and a shade more difficult in its execution. We have studied the subject a great deal, and we think the best way is to throw yourself out, and trust to chance for alighting on your feet. If you make the driver alight first, and then throw yourself upon him, you will find that he breaks your fall materially. In the event of your contemplating an offer of eightpence, on no account make the tender, or show the money, until you are safely on the pavement. It is very bad policy attempting to save the fourpence. You are very much in the power of a cabman, and he considers it a kind of fee not to do you any wilful damage. Any instruction, however, in the art of getting out of a cab is wholly unnecessary if you are going any distance, because the probability is that you will be shot lightly out before you have completed the third mile.

We are not aware of any instance on record in which a cab-horse has performed three consecutive miles without going down once. What of that? It is all excitement. And in these days of derangement of the nervous system and universal lassitude, people are content to pay handsomely for excitement; where can it be procured at a cheaper rate?

But to return to the red cab; it was omnipresent. You had but to walk down Holborn, or Fleet Street, or any of the principal thoroughfares in which there is a great deal of traffic, and judge for yourself. You had hardly turned into the street, when you saw a trunk or two, lying on the ground: an uprooted post, a hat-box, a portmanteau, and a carpet-bag, strewed about in a very picturesque manner: a horse in a cab standing by, looking about him with great unconcern; and a crowd, shouting and screaming with delight, cooling their flushed faces against the glass windows of a chemist's shop.—"What's the matter here, can you tell me?"— "On'y a cab, sir."—"Anybody hurt, do you know?"— "On'y the fare, sir. I see him a-turnin' the corner, and

I ses to another gen'lm'n 'that's a reg'lar little oss that, and he's a-comin' along rayther sweet, an't he?'—'He just is,' ses the other gen'lm'n, ven bump they cums agin the post, and out flies the fare like bricks." Need we say it was the red cab; or that the gentleman with the straw in his mouth, who emerged so coolly from the chemist's shop and philosophically climbing into the little dickey, started off at full gallop, was the red cab's licensed driver?

The ubiquity of this red cab, and the influence it exercised over the risible muscles of justice itself, was perfectly astonishing. You walked into the justice-room of the Mansion House; the whole court resounded with merriment. The Lord Mayor threw himself back in his chair, in a state of frantic delight at his own joke; every vein in Mr. Hobler's countenance was swollen with laughter, partly at the Lord Mayor's facetiousness, but more at his own; the constables and police-officers' were (as in duty bound) in ecstasies, at Mr. Hobler and the Lord Mayor combined; and the very paupers, glancing respectfully at the beadle's countenance, tried to smile, as even he relaxed. A tall, weazen-faced man, with an impediment in his speech, would be endeavouring to state a case of imposition against the red cab's driver, and the red cab's driver, and the Lord Mayor, and Mr. Hobler, would be having a little fun among themselves, to the inordinate delight of everybody but the complainant. In the end, justice would be so tickled with the red-cab driver's native humour, that the fine would be mitigated, and he would go away full gallop, in the red cab, to impose on somebody else without loss of time.

The driver of the red cab, confident in the strength of his moral principles, like many other philosophers,

THE LAST CAB-DRIVER

was wont to set the feelings and opinions of society at complete defiance. Generally speaking, perhaps, he would as soon carry a fare safely to his destination as he would upset him—sooner, perhaps, because in that case he not only got the money, but had the additional amusement of running a longer heat against some smart rival. But society made war upon him in the shape of penalties, and he must make war upon society in his own way. This was the reasoning of the red-cab driver. So he bestowed a searching look upon the fare, as he put his hand in his waistcoat-pocket, when he had gone half the mile, to get the money ready; and if he brought forth eightpence, out he went.

The last time we saw our friend was one wet evening in Tottenham Court Road, when he was engaged in a very warm and somewhat personal altercation with a loquacious little gentleman in a green coat. Poor fellow! there were great excuses to be made for him: he had not received above eighteenpence more than his fare, and consequently laboured under a great deal of very natural indignation. The dispute had attained a pretty considerable height, when at last the loquacious little gentleman, making a mental calculation of the distance, and finding that he had already paid more than he ought, avowed his unalterable determination to "pull up" the cabman in the morning.

"Now, just mark this, young man," said the little gentleman, "I'll pull you up to-morrow morning."

"No; will you though?" said our friend, with a sneer.

"I will," replied the little gentleman, "mark my words, that's all. If I live till to-morrow morning, you shall repent this."

There was a steadiness of purpose, and indignation of speech, about the little gentleman, as he took an angry pinch of snuff, after this last declaration, which made a visible impression on the mind of the red-cab driver. He appeared to hesitate for an instant. It was only for an instant; his resolve was soon taken.

"You'll pull me up, will you?" said our friend.

"I will," rejoined the little gentleman, with even greater vehemence than before.

"Very well," said our friend, tucking up his shirt-sleeves very calmly. "There'll be three veeks for that. Wery good; that'll bring me up to the middle o' next month. Three veeks more would carry me on to my birthday, and then I've got ten pound to draw. I may as well get board, lodgin', and washin', till then, out of the county, as pay for it myself; consequently here goes!"

So, without more ado, the red-cab driver knocked the little gentleman down, and then called the police to take himself into custody, with all the civility in the world.

A story is nothing without the sequel; and therefore, we may state that to our certain knowledge, the board, lodging, and washing, were all provided in due course. We happen to know the fact, for it came to our knowledge thus: We went over the House of Correction for the county of Middlesex shortly after, to witness the operation of the silent system; and looked on all the "wheels" with the greatest anxiety, in search of our long-lost friend. He was nowhere to be seen, however, and we began to think that the little gentleman in the green coat must have relented, when, as we were tra-versing the kitchen-garden, which lies in a sequestered part of the prison, we were startled by hearing a voice, which apparently proceeded from the wall, pouring forth its soul in the plaintive air of "All round my hat," which was then just beginning to form a recognised portion of our national music.

We started.—"What voice is that?" said we.

The Governor shook his head.

"Sad fellow," he replied, "very sad. He positively refused to work on the wheel; so, after many trials, I was compelled to order him into solitary confinement. He says he likes it very much though, and I am afraid he does, for he lies on his back on the floor, and sings comic songs all day!"

Shall we add that our heart had not deceived us; and that the comic singer was no other than our eagerly-sought friend, the red-cab driver?

We have never seen him since, but we have strong reason to suspect that this noble individual was a distant relative of a waterman of our acquaintance, who, on one occasion, when we were passing the coach-stand over which he presides, after standing very quietly to see a tall man struggle into a cab, ran up very briskly when it was all over (as his brethren invariably do), and, touching his hat, asked, as a matter of course, for "a copper for the waterman." Now, the fare was by no means a handsome man; and, waxing very indignant at the demand, he replied—"Money! What for? Coming up and looking at me, I suppose?"—"Veil, sir," rejoined the waterman, with a smile of immovable complacency, "*That's* worth twopence."

This identical waterman afterwards attained a very prominent station in society; and as we know something of his life, and have often thought of telling what we *do* know, perhaps we shall never have a better opportunity than the present.

Mr. William Barker, then, for that was the gentleman's name, Mr. William Barker was born—but why need we relate where Mr. William Barker was born, or when? Why scrutinise the entries in parochial ledgers, or seek to penetrate the Lucinian mysteries of lying-in hospitals? Mr. William Barker *was* born, or he had never been. There is a son—there was a father. There is an effect—there was a cause. Surely this is sufficient information for the most Fatima-like curiosity; and, if it be not, we regret our inability to supply any further evidence on the point. Can there be a more satisfactory, or more strictly parliamentary course? Impossible.

We at once avow a similar inability to record at what precise period, or by what particular process, this gentleman's patronymic, of William Barker, became corrupted into "Bill Boorker." Mr. Barker acquired a high standing, and no inconsiderable reputation, among the members of that profession to which he more peculiarly devoted his energies; and to them he was generally known, either by the familiar appellation of "Bill Boorker," or the flattering designation of "Aggerawatin' Bill," the latter being a playful and expressive *sobriquet*, illustrative of Mr. Barker's great talent in "aggerawatin'" and rendering wild such subjects of her Majesty as are conveyed from place to place through the instrumentality of omnibuses. Of the early life of Mr. Barker little is known, and even that little is involved in considerable doubt and obscurity. A want of application, a restlessness of purpose, a thirsting after porter, a love of all that is roving and cadger-like in nature, shared in common with many other great geniuses, appear to have been his leading characteristics. The busy hum of a parochial free-school, and the shady repose of a county jail, were alike inefficacious in producing the slightest alteration in Mr. Barker's disposition. His feverish attachment to change and variety nothing could repress; his native daring no punishment could subdue.

If Mr. Barker can be fairly said to have had any weakness in his earlier years, it was an amiable one—love; love in its most comprehensive form—a love of ladies, liquids, and pocket-handkerchiefs. It was no selfish feeling; it was not confined to his own possessions, which but too many men regard with exclusive complacency. No; it was a nobler love—a general principle. It extended itself with equal force to the property of other people.

There is something very affecting in this. It is still more affecting to know that such philanthropy is but imperfectly rewarded. Bow Street, Newgate, and Millbank, are a poor return for general benevolence, evincing itself in an irrepressible love for all created objects. Mr. Barker felt it so. After a lengthened interview with the highest legal authorities, he quitted his ungrateful country, with the consent, and at the expense, of its Government; proceeded to a distant shore; and there employed himself, like another Cincinnatus, in clearing and cultivating the soil—a peaceful pursuit, in which a term of seven years glided almost imperceptibly away.

Whether, at the expiration of the period we have just mentioned, the British Government required Mr. Barker's presence here, or did not require his residence abroad, we have no distinct means of ascertaining. We should be inclined, however, to favour the latter position, inasmuch as we do not find that he was advanced to any other public post on his return, than the post at the corner of the Haymarket, where he officiated as assistant-waterman to the hackney-coach-stand. Seated, in this capacity, on a couple of tubs near the curb-stone, with a brass plate and number suspended round his neck by a massive chain, and his ankles curiously enveloped in haybands, he is supposed to have made those observations on human nature which exercised so material an influence over all his proceedings in later life.

Mr. Barker had not officiated for many months in this capacity when the appearance of the first omnibus caused the public mind to go in a new direction, and prevented a great many hackney-coaches from going in any direction at all. The genius of Mr. Barker at once perceived the whole extent of the injury that would be eventually inflicted on cab and coach stands, and, by consequence, on watermen also, by the progress of the system of which the first omnibus was a part. He saw, too, the necessity of adopting some more profitable profession; and his active mind at once perceived how much might be done in the way of enticing the youthful and unwary, and shoving the old and helpless, into the wrong bus, and carrying them off, until, reduced to despair, they ransomed themselves by the payment of sixpence a head, or, to adopt his own figurative expression in all its native beauty, "till they was rig'larly done over, and forked out the stumpy."

An opportunity for realising his fondest anticipations soon presented itself. Rumours were rife on the hackney-coach-stands that a bus was building, to run from Lisson Grove to the Bank, down Oxford Street and Holborn; and the rapid increase of buses on the Paddington Road encouraged the idea. Mr. Barker secretly and cautiously inquired in the proper quarters. The report was correct; the "Royal William" was to make its first journey on the following Monday. It was a crack affair altogether. An enterprising young cabman, of established reputation as a dashing whip—for he had compromised with the parents of three scrunched children, and just "worked out" his fine, for knocking down an old lady—was the driver; and the spirited proprietor, knowing Mr. Barker's qualifications, appointed him to the vacant office of cad on the very first application. The bus began to run, and Mr. Barker entered into a new suit of clothes, and on a new sphere of action.

To recapitulate all the improvements introduced by this extraordinary man into the omnibus system— gradually, indeed, but surely—would occupy a far greater space than we are enabled to devote to this imperfect memoir. To him is universally assigned the original suggestion of the practice which afterwards became so general—of the driver of a second bus keeping constantly behind the first one, and driving the pole of his vehicle either into the door of the other, every time it was opened, or through the body of any lady or gentleman who might make an attempt to get into it; a humorous and pleasant invention, exhibiting all that originality of idea, and fine bold flow of spirits, so conspicuous in every action of this great man.

Mr. Barker had opponents of course; what man in public life has not? But even his worst enemies cannot deny that he has taken more old ladies and gentlemen to Paddington who wanted to go to the Bank, and more old ladies and gentlemen to the Bank who wanted to go to Paddington, than any six men on the road; and however much malevolent spirits may pretend to doubt the accuracy of the statement, they well know it to be an established fact that he has forcibly conveyed a variety of ancient persons of either sex, to both places, who had not the slightest or most distant intention of going anywhere at all.

Mr. Barker was the identical cad who nobly distinguished himself, some time since by keeping a trades-man on the step—the omnibus going at full speed all the time—till he had thrashed him to his entire satisfaction, and finally throwing him away, when he had quite done with him. Mr. Barker it *ought* to have been, who honestly indignant at being ignominiously ejected from a house of public entertainment, kicked the landlord in the knee, and thereby caused his death. We say it *ought* to have been Mr. Barker, because the action was not a common one, and could have emanated from no ordinary mind.

It has now become matter of history; it is recorded in the Newgate Calendar; and we wish we could attribute this piece of daring heroism to Mr. Barker. We regret being compelled to state that it was not performed by him. Would, for the family credit we could add, that it was achieved by his brother!

It was in the exercise of the nicer details of his profession that Mr. Barker's knowledge of human nature was beautifully displayed. He could tell at a glance where a passenger wanted to go to, and would shout the name of the place accordingly, without the slightest reference to the real destination of the vehicle. He knew exactly the kind of old lady that would be too much flurried by the process of pushing in and pulling out of the caravan, to discover where she had been put down, until too late; had an intuitive perception of what was passing in a passenger's mind when he inwardly resolved to "pull that cad up to-morrow morning"; and never failed to make himself agreeable to female servants, whom he would place next the door, and talk to all the way.

Human judgment is never infallible, and it would occasionally happen that Mr. Barker experimentalised with the timidity or forbearance of the wrong person, in which case a summons to a police-office was, on more than one occasion, followed by a committal to prison. It was not in the power of trifles such as these, however, to subdue the freedom of his spirit. As soon as they passed away, he resumed the duties of his profession with unabated ardour.

We have spoken of Mr. Barker and of the red-cab driver in the past tense. Alas! Mr. Barker has again become an absentee; and the class of men to which they both belonged are fast disappearing. Improvement has peered beneath the aprons of our cabs, and penetrated to the very innermost recesses of our omnibuses. Dirt and fustian will vanish before cleanliness and livery. Slang will be forgotten when civility becomes general: and that enlightened, eloquent, sage, and profound body, the Magistracy of London, will be deprived of half their amusement, and half their occupation.

"Richard the Third.—Duke of Glo'ster, 2*l.*; Earl of Richmond, 1*l.*; Duke of Buckingham, 15*s.*; Catesby, 12*s.*; Tressel, 10*s.* 6*d.*; Lord Stanley, 5*s.*; Lord Mayor of London, 2*s.* 6*d.*"

Such are the written placards wafered up in the gentlemen's dressing-room, in the green-room (where there is any), at a private theatre; and such are the sums extracted from the shop-till, or overcharged in the office expenditure, by the donkeys who are prevailed upon to pay for permission to exhibit their lamentable ignorance and boobyism on the stage of a private theatre. This they do, in proportion to the scope afforded by the character for the display of their imbecility. For instance, the Duke of Glo'ster is well worth two pounds, because he has it all to himself; he must wear a real sword, and what is better still, he must draw it several times in the course of the piece. The soliloquies alone are well worth fifteen shillings; then there is the stabbing King Henry—decidedly cheap at three-and-sixpence, that's eighteen-and-sixpence; bullying the coffin-bearers— say eighteenpence, though it's worth much more— that's a pound. Then the love scene with Lady Anne, and the bustle of the fourth act can't be dear at ten shillings more—that's only one pound ten, including the "off with his head!"—which is sure to bring down the applause, and it is very easy to do—"Orf with his ed" (very quick and loud;—then slow and sneeringly)—

"So much for Bu-u-u-uckingham!" Lay the emphasis on the "uck"; get yourself gradually into a corner, and work with your right hand, while you're saying it, as if you were feeling your way, and it's sure to do. The tent scene is confessedly worth half-a-sovereign, and so you have the fight in, gratis, and everybody knows what an effect may be produced by a good combat. One—two—three—four—over; then, one—two—three—four—under; then thrust; then dodge and slide about; then fall down on one knee; then fight upon it, and then get up again and stagger. You may keep on doing this, as long as it seems to take—say ten minutes—and then fall down (backwards, if you can manage it without hurting yourself), and die game: nothing like it for producing an effect. They always do it at Astley's and Sadler's Wells, and if they don't know how to do this sort of thing, who in the world does? A small child, or a female in white, increases the interest of a combat materially—indeed, we are not aware that a regular legitimate terrific broadsword combat could be done without; but it would be rather difficult, and somewhat unusual, to introduce this effect in the last scene of *Richard the Third*, so the only thing to be done is just to make the best of a bad bargain, and be as long as possible fighting it out.

The principal patrons of private theatres are dirty boys, low copying-clerks in attorneys' offices, capacious-headed youths from City counting-houses, Jews whose business, as lenders of fancy dresses, is a sure passport to the amateur stage, shop-boys who now and then mistake their masters' money for their own; and a choice miscellany of idle vagabonds. The proprietor of a private theatre may be an ex-scene-painter, a low coffee-house-keeper, a disappointed eighth-rate actor, a retired smuggler, or uncertificated bankrupt. The theatre itself may be in Catherine Street, Strand, the purlieus of the city, the neighbourhood of Gray's Inn Lane, or the vicinity of Sadler's Wells; or it may, perhaps, form the chief nuisance of some shabby street, on the Surrey side of Waterloo Bridge.

The lady performers pay nothing for their characters, and, it is needless to add, are usually selected from one class of society; the audiences are necessarily of much the same character as the performers, who receive, in return for their contributions to the management, tickets to the amount of the money they pay.

All the minor theatres in London, especially the lowest, constitute the centre of a little stage-struck neighbourhood. Each of them has an audience exclusively its own; and at any you will see dropping into the pit at half-price, or swaggering into the back of a box, if the price of admission be a reduced one, divers boys of from fifteen to twenty-one years of age, who throw back their coat and turn up their wristbands, after the portraits of Count D'Orsay, hum tunes and whistle when the curtain is down, by way of persuading the people near them that they are not at all anxious to have it up again, and speak familiarly of the inferior performers as Bill Such-a-one, and Ned So-and-so, or tell each other how a new piece called *The Unknown Bandit of the Invisible Cavern* is in rehearsal; how Mister Palmer is to play the Unknown Bandit; how Charley Scarton is to take the part of an English sailor, and fight a broadsword combat with six unknown bandits, at one and the same time (one theatrical sailor is always equal to half-a-dozen men at least); how Mister Palmer and Charley Scarton are to go through a double hornpipe in fetters in the second act; how the interior of the invisible cavern is to occupy the whole extent of the stage; and other town-surprising theatrical announcements. These gentlemen are the amateurs—the Richards, Shylocks, Beverleys, and Othellos—the Young Dorntons, Rovers, Captain Absolutes, and Charles Surfaces—of a private theatre.

See them at the neighbouring public-house or the theatrical coffee-shop! They are the kings of the place, supposing no real performers to be present; and roll about, hats on one side, and arms akimbo, as if they had actually come into possession of eighteen shillings a week, and a share of a ticket night. If one of them does but know an Astley's supernumerary he is a happy fellow. The mingled air of envy and admiration with which his companions will regard him, as he converses familiarly with some mouldy-looking man in a fancy neckerchief, whose partially corked eyebrows, and half-rouged face, testify to the fact of his having just left the stage or the circle, sufficiently shows in what high admiration these public characters are held.

With the double view of guarding against the discovery of friends or employers, and enhancing the interest of an assumed character, by attaching a high-sounding name to its representative, these geniuses assume fictitious names, which are not the least amusing part of the play-bill of a private theatre. Belville, Melville, Treville, Berkeley, Randolph, Byron, St. Clair, and so forth, are among the humblest; and the less imposing titles of Jenkins, Walker, Thomson, Barker, Solomons, &c., are completely laid aside. There is something imposing in this, and it is an excellent apology for shabbiness into the bargain. A shrunken, faded coat, a decayed hat, a patched and soiled pair of trousers—nay, even a very dirty shirt (and none of these appearances are very uncommon among the members of the *corps dramatique*), may be worn for the purpose of disguise, and to prevent the remotest chance of recognition. Then it prevents any troublesome inquiries or explanations about employment land pursuits; everybody is a gentleman at large, for the occasion, and there are none of those unpleasant and unnecessary distinctions to which even genius must occasionally succumb elsewhere. As to the ladies (God bless them), they are quite above any formal absurdities; the mere circumstance of your being behind the scenes is a sufficient introduction to their society—for of course they know that none but strictly respectable persons would be admitted into that close fellowship with them which acting engenders. They place implicit reliance on the manager, no doubt; and as to the manager, he is all affability when he knows you well—or, in other words, when he has pocketed your money once, and entertains confident hopes of doing so again.

A quarter before eight—there will be a full house to-night—six parties in the boxes, already; four little boys and a woman in the pit; and two fiddles and a flute in the orchestra, who have got through five overtures since seven o'clock (the hour fixed for the commence-ment of the performances), and have just begun the sixth. There will be plenty of it, though, when it does begin, for there is enough in the bill to last six hours at least.

That gentleman in the white hat and checked shirt, brown coat and brass buttons, lounging behind the stage-box on the O. P. side, is Mr. Horatio St. Julien, alias Jem Larkins. His line is genteel comedy—his father's, coal and potato. He *does* Alfred Highflier in the last piece, and very well he'll do it—at the price. The party of gentlemen in the opposite box, to whom he has just nodded, are friends and supporters of Mr. Beverley (otherwise Loggins), the Macbeth of the night. You observe their attempts to appear easy and gentlemanly, each member of the party with his feet cocked upon the cushion in front of the box! They let them do these things here, upon the same humane principle which permits poor people's children to knock double-knocks at the door of an empty house—because they can't do it anywhere else. The two stout men in the centre box, with an opera-glass ostentatiously placed before them, are friends of the proprietor—opulent country managers, as he confidentially informs every individual among the crew behind the curtain—opulent country managers looking out for recruits; a representation which Mr. Nathan, the dresser, who is in the manager's interest, and has just arrived with the costumes, offers to confirm upon oath if required—corroborative evidence, however, is quite unnecessary, for the gulls believe it at once.

The stout Jewess who has just entered is the mother of the pale bony little girl, with the necklace of blue glass beads, sitting by her; she is being brought up to "the profession." Pantomime is to be her line, and she is coming out to-night, in a hornpipe after the tragedy. The short thin man beside Mr. St. Julien, whose white face is so deeply seared with the small-pox, and whose dirty shirt-front is inlaid with open-work, and embossed with coral studs like ladybirds, is the low comedian and comic singer of the establishment. The remainder of the audience—a tolerably numerous one by this time—are a motley group of dupes and blackguards.

The foot-lights have just made their appearance: the wicks of the six little oil-lamps round the only tier of boxes are being turned up, and the additional light thus afforded serves to show the presence of dirt, and absence of paint, which form a prominent feature in the audience part of the house. As these preparations, however, announce the speedy commencement of the play, let us take a peep "behind," previous to the ringing-up.

The little narrow passages beneath the stage are neither especially clean nor too brilliantly lighted; and the absence of any flooring, together with the damp mildewy smell which pervades the place, does not conduce in any great degree to their comfortable appearance. Don't fall over this plate-basket—it's one of the "properties"—the cauldron for the witches' cave; and the three uncouth-looking figures, with broken clothes-props in their hands, who are drinking gin-and-water out of a pint pot, are the weird sisters. This miserable room, lighted by candles in sconces placed at lengthened intervals round the wall, is the dressing-room, common to the gentlemen performers, and the square hole in the ceiling is *the* trap-door of the stage above. You will observe that the ceiling is ornamented with the beams that support the boards, and tastefully hung with cobwebs.

The characters in the tragedy are all dressed, and their own clothes are scattered in hurried confusion over the wooden dresser which surrounds the room. That snuff-shop-looking figure, in front of the glass, is Banquo: and the young lady with the liberal display of legs, who is kindly painting his face with a hare's foot, is dressed for Fleance. The large woman, who is consulting the stage directions in Cumberland's edition of *Macbeth*, is the Lady Macbeth of the night; she is always selected to play the part, because she is tall and stout, and *looks* a little like Mrs. Siddons—at a

George Cruikshank

PRIVATE THEATRES

considerable distance. That stupid-looking milksop, with light hair and bow legs—a kind of man whom you can warrant town-made—is fresh caught; he plays Malcolm to-night, just to accustom himself to an audience. He will get on better by degrees; he will play Othello in a month, and in a month more will very probably be apprehended on a charge of embezzlement. The black-eyed female with whom he is talking so earnestly, is dressed for the "gentlewoman." It is *her* first appearance, too—in that character. The boy of fourteen who is having his eyebrows smeared with soap and whitening, is Duncan, King of Scotland; and the two dirty men with the corked countenances, in very old green tunics, and dirty drab boots, are the "army."

"Look sharp below there, gents," exclaims the dresser, a red-headed and red-whiskered Jew, calling through the trap, "they're a-going to ring up. The flute says he'll be blowed if he plays any more, and they're getting precious noisy in front." A general rush immediately takes place to the half-dozen little steep steps leading to the stage, and the heterogeneous group are soon assembled at the side scenes, in breathless anxiety and motley confusion.

"Now," cries the manager, consulting the written list which hangs behind the first P. S. wing, "Scene 1, open country—lamps down—thunder and lightning—all ready, White?" [This is addressed to one of the army.] "All ready."—"Very well. Scene 2, front chamber. Is the front chamber down?"—? "Yes."—"Very well."—"Jones" [to the other army who is up in the flies]. "Hallo!"—"Wind up the open country when we ring up."—"I'll take care."—"Scene 3, back perspective with practical bridge. Bridge ready, White? Got the tressels there?"—"All right."

"Very well. Clear the stage," cries the manager, hastily packing every member of the company into the little space there is between the wings and the wall, and one wing and another. "Places, places. Now then, Witches—Duncan—Malcolm—bleeding officer—where's the bleeding officer?"—"Here!" replies the officer, who has been rose-pinking for the character. "Get ready, then; now, White, ring the second music-bell." The actors who are to be discovered are hastily arranged, and the actors who are not to be discovered place themselves, in their anxiety to peep at the house, just where the audience can see them. The bell rings, and the orchestra, in acknowledgement of the call, play three distinct chords. The bell rings—the tragedy (!) opens—and our description closes.

GLOSSARY

ALDERMAN WAITHMAN'S MONUMENT
An obelisk in Salisbury Square, erected in memory of
Robert Waithman, who died in 1833. He was a former
Member of Parliament and Lord Mayor of London
from 1823–24.

ALMACK'S
Almack's Assembly Rooms was a high society social
club that operated in London from 1765–1871. It was
one of the first clubs to admit both men and women.

ASTLEY'S
Situated in Westminster Bridge Road, Astley's Amphi-
theatre was a performance space for theatricals, and a
circus.

BEDLAM
The Bethlem Hospital for the insane in St George's
Fields, Lambeth. The site now houses the Imperial War
Museum, which was opened in 1936.

CHANCERY
A civil court which dealt with wills and debtors, it was
abolished in 1875.

CLARE MARKET
A maze of narrow Elizabethan streets housing a market
of butchers' shops and greengrocers. The area was re-
developed in 1900 and is now a campus of the London
School of Economics.

Copenhagen House

A famous tavern and tea house that operated in Islington from the early seventeenth century until 1855.

Covent Garden

Formerly London's wholesale fruit and vegetable market, now a popular shopping and tourist destination, and home to the Royal Opera House.

'Dials'

Seven Dials, a notorious slum or 'rookery', which took its name from the point where seven streets converged. Today it is part of London's West End and a fashionable shopping district.

Duke of York's Column

A monument to Prince Frederick, Duke of York (1763–1827), the second son of George III, who is immortalised in the nursery rhyme 'The Grand Old Duke of York'. It stands between Waterloo Place and the Mall.

Guildhall

The City's only surviving secular medieval building, dating from 1411. It stands on Gresham Street and is still home of the City of London Corporation, acting as a setting for banquets for visiting heads of state and other dignitaries.

Hammersmith Suspension Bridge

The first suspension bridge to cross the River Thames, it was opened in 1827 and operated for over fifty years before concerns about its safety necessitated its replacement in 1887.

Holywell Street

Holywell Street was situated parallel with the Strand, and was the centre for the sale of pornography – as well as clothes – in Victorian times. It was demolished in 1900 so that the Strand could be widened.

HOUSE OF CORRECTION
Coldbath Fields Prison in the Mount Pleasant area of Clerkenwell; it housed prisoners on short sentences of two years or less. The prison was closed in 1877 and the site now belongs to the Post Office.

LLOYD'S
The home of London's insurance brokers, originally housed in Lloyd's Coffee House in the 1680s. At the time of Dickens's writing it was situated in the Royal Exchange opposite the Bank of England.

MARSH GATE
A toll gate on the Surrey Turnpike in what is now Waterloo Bridge Road.

MONMOUTH STREET
One of the seven streets forming Seven Dials. Known in Dickens's time for selling second-hand clothes, it is still in situ today.

NEWGATE
London's principal prison, where public executions were carried out until 1868. Although he was opposed to the death penalty, Dickens attended the hanging of François Benjamin Courvoisier in 1840, taking a room in the Magpie and Stump, overlooking the gallows. The public house is still there.

OBELISK IN ST GEORGE'S FIELDS
The obelisk at St George's Circus, Southwark, was built in 1771 in honour of Brass Crosby (1725–93), a former Member of Parliament and Lord Mayor of London.

OLD BAILEY

London's main criminal court, adjacent to Newgate prison. When Newgate was demolished in 1904 the present Old Bailey was built on the site. Today it tries the most serious crimes.

PENITENTIARY

The National Penitentiary in Millbank, Pimlico. It was open from 1816–90. The site now houses several significant buildings, including the Tate Britain gallery.

'RED-US'

The Red House at Battersea, demolished in 1850, was a tavern infamous for petty theft, brawling and debauchery.

'ROOKERY'

A colloquial term for a slum that was derived from a perceived similarity with the sprawling, noisy colonies of multiple nests that rooks – a bird in the crow family – inhabit.

SADLER'S WELLS

A theatre and performing arts venue. In Dickens's time it sometimes presented adaptations of popular novels, including his *A Christmas Carol* and *The Old Curiosity Shop*, which ran during January 1841. It is now principally used for ballet and opera.

SESSIONS HOUSE

The Sessions House, Clerkenwell Green, served as the most urban and senior magistrates' centre of Middlesex. The building is now a private members' club.

ST PAUL'S CHURCHYARD

In the precincts of St Paul's Cathedral. Known for the

number of booksellers who traded there in Dickens's time.

WHITE CONDUIT HOUSE
A large public house in what is now Penton Street, Islington, that was popular with the lower orders of society. It was demolished in 1849.

MACMILLAN COLLECTOR'S LIBRARY

Own the world's great works of literature in one beautiful collectible library

Designed and curated to appeal to book lovers everywhere, Macmillan Collector's Library editions are small enough to travel with you and striking enough to take pride of place on your bookshelf. These much-loved literary classics also make the perfect gift.

Beautifully produced with gilt edges, a ribbon marker, bespoke illustrated cover and real cloth binding, every Macmillan Collector's Library hardback adheres to the same high production values.

Discover something new or cherish your favourite stories with this elegant collection.

Macmillan Collector's Library: own, collect, and treasure

Discover the full range at
macmillancollectorslibrary.com